DOPE GIRL 4

Acknowledgements

First and foremost I want to praise and thank my Lord for absolutely everything. It's not possible to count His favors and blessings, so I won't even try. Instead I thank Him for everything.

Next, the ladies of my life: my wife Jennah, Mom Diedra, Grandma Rainey, daughters Bryonna and Jessica, and my granddaughters Aliya and Liv.

My man's and dem: my sons, grandson, brothers, cousins and err body else.

And of course all of y'all, the readers.... Athea Cranford, Ghoul Field, LaKeysa, Shine, Diana S., Cassandra Hayes, Myijai, Karen Taylor, Tammy Powell Herbert, Toshiba, Shanika, Denise Miller, Love, cssmlf@yahoo.com, Miss Keshia Henry, Byron Mathis, Rosie, Damion Hamilton, Tanisha Barrett, Tisha Wills, Lakeshia, Rhonda, Malisha Marie Jones, Saima Mann, Gwendolyn Allen Lawson G Law, Laurie Starr Thomas, Patryce Johnson, Clarice MsRere Henry, Chef Brooklyn Shandy, Amie, Aisha Berry, Kastin Blak, Missy Yel, Stacey Michelle Hunt, Cynt Lil Cuba Lady Aces SC prez, CeCe Lucas, Marcel Ford, Tanisha Reed, Karimah, Tee Tee Aintworriedaboutdanext Samuels, Stacey Nelson, LaVina Richardson, Betty Imthatdamngood Bethea, Antoinette Mitchell Tate, Imanni Bella Angel Gaye, Rebecca Ortiz, Areya Square, Krystal Johnson, Rashida, Sarah Clowers, Tasha Williams, Helena Harris, Niecy Niece Tyson, LaShawn Green, Lissha, Iona Sawyer, Jerrice Owens, Troi Thompson, Anissa, Shandi obsessedwithpurple Guibeaux, Liltinybk Williams Liltinybk Williams, Neice Sanders, Tammy Jernigan, Author Sunshine, Felicia Coleman Brown, Yolanda Evans Harris, Benita Williams, Lera Murray, Enez Welch, Dion E Cheese@iurban.org, Denise Moore, Sylina Freeman, Stephanie Thompson, Natasha Potts, Kim Fonda, Tonya Everett, Kateri Young,

Lisa Bryant, LaShonna Tinner Gross, Bernie Bagley, Anita Guerra, Yolanda R. Ray, Sharon LadyShay, Jacque (JJ) Jones, Patricia Watkins, NeKesha Milton, Kimberly Carter, Michelle Wilson, Latonya Lady-Blaize Knight, Kayla MeBendez, AbdulHaqq, Meaka Imperfectbeauty Garner, Vanessa Speaks, Tamisha Daunyale Scruggs, Kathleen Lucas, Priscilla Murray, Pista Pete, Monique Colter, Alicia Jel-lo Dean, Cheryl Kitchen Lewis, Lisa Saxon, and Bree. Thanks for all of your loyal support, encouragement, suggestions, and love. Team Salaam!!!!

"Treat women nicely, for a woman is created from a rib, and the most curved portion of the rib is its upper portion, so, if you should try to straighten it, it will break, but if you leave it as it is, it will remain crooked. So treat women nicely"

Introduction

"Ok look it, you can look, and touch as much as you like; just don't be tryna put no fangers in her. And if 'n you can't put no fanger in her then you damn sho cain't put yo' thang off in her!" Kathy said emphatically. Molesting her daughter came with rules.

Tywanna just lay there in a cheap flannel nightgown covering her frail eight-year-old frame. Her eyes were tightly shut in hopes that this latest pervert would have a flash of humanity and leave her alone. Just let the little girl sleep and go home to their wife. If not then it was a trap.

Her mind flashed back a couple of years to when she had come across a young possum. She quickly decided the small rodent would be a nice addition to the variety of animals that called the Johnson residence home. Every stray cat and dog knew it could at least get a bowl of fresh water if it happened by, food too on the rare occasion that Tywanna had had her fill.

The small possum would fit right in the mini zoo young Tywanna ran. The family of squirrels, chickens, and roosters were her family and only friends.

The only problem with the plan was that the critter preferred the woods to whatever the girl was offering. For all it knew the strange creature wanted to eat her. The possum ran, ducked, and dodged in a valiant effort not to get captured, but ultimately got cornered.

With no place to run or chance of escape, the poor thing keeled over on its back and died. Tywanna was devastated by the turn of events.

"Aww," the young girl whined as she scooped the dead animal into her hands. Tears streamed down her face as she mourned its short life. She cradled it and rocked gently in her sorrow.

Suddenly the possum came back to life. It opened its eyes along with its mouth full of razor sharp teeth. Before Tywanna could drop

3

the ferocious hissing little beast, it clamped down on the flesh between her thumb and index finger.

"You little bitch!" she screamed flailing her hand to free herself from the savage animal. 'Little bitch' was a term she picked up from her mother.

Anytime her child interfered with what she had going on, like smoking crack or fucking and sucking to get crack, Kathy cursed her daughter.

When the animal's teeth finally met through the flesh of its victim a final thrust sent it sailing into a pine tree.

Tywanna was bleeding profusely and in incredible pain but more than anything, she was angry. Mad as hell actually, as she approached the dazed rodent. It struggled to regain its composure so it could scurry into the woods and find safety but didn't make it.

Tywanna pounced before the possum had a chance to fully recover. Using a garden tool, she beat the animal to pieces. Not quite finished she kicked the parts in different directions until they were dispersed into the woods.

The young girl learned two very valuable lessons that day. The first was how to 'play possum' to lure your opponent in by pretending to be sick or weak and then when you had them close enough to kill, KILL!

The second lesson was that payback was sweet.

Chapter 1

"What the hell?" Angela cursed in English and then ranted in Spanish at the high beams flashing in her rearview mirror. She had recognized the SUV as one of the security teams and pulled over. She assumed he was trailing her for her safety, but nothing could be further from the truth.

The woman deemed the help as beneath her and spoke down to them if and when she spoke to them. She gathered a mouthful of venom to spit at him for interrupting her mission. Angela was quite proud of herself for standing up to Mama Salazar. The woman had a reputation for being a very dangerous woman. Still she stood her ground and was ready to reveal to Juan that Cameisha was his sister.

Angela snatched her car over to the curb abruptly and rolled down the window. She was ready to read El-Capitan the riot act as he approached. Only the vicious man didn't do nagging. As soon as he reached the driver's side window, he lifted the silenced pistol and fired twice. The muted gunshot redecorated the cream leather interior pink with blood and brain matter. He smiled down at his handiwork and turned on his heels.

"It is done," El-Capitan reported when Marisol took his call.

"Bueno, Bueno," she nodded as a black hearted smile wrinkled her face. This would start a war that would rid the world of the shame of her beloved husband's illegitimate child. A war she knew she would win. However, pride comes before the fall.

****

"Hmm," Juan muttered when he awoke alone in his bed. Had his sexy girlfriend been home he would have rolled over and slid his morning erection inside of her. Nothing starts the day off like busting a good nut.

"Angela!" he called towards the bathroom and got no reply. He got the same results as he called her name throughout the unit. His fingers snapped recalling her telling him she was going to see his mother the night before.

He remembered thinking it odd since his mother didn't particularly care for Angela and Angela didn't like anyone. He shrugged it off assuming they were trying to make nice for his sake. Juan could be gullible like that when it came to those two.

Juan grabbed his phone to call but changed his mind. Instead, he decided to drive over and treat his women to breakfast. He selected an outfit from his closet and then selected a vehicle. The gate opened at the mansion and he drove in. A frown furrowed his brown when Angela's car wasn't among the fleet of luxury cars in the circular driveway.

"Hola Mama, donde esta mi espousa?" Juan asked after greeting his mother with a kiss on her fleshy cheek.

"Tu espousa?" she scoffed indignantly. "No esta aki. She went to see the black girl."

"Cameisha?" Juan frowned deeper. That was even odder to him.

"Si, they were arguing on the phone last night and she went to her house. I hope that black girl hasn't done anything to her," Marisol moaned crossing her chest. She then lifted her crucifix to her lips and kissed it for added drama, with her dramatic ass.

"On the phone?" Juan asked as he pulled his from his pocket. His mother was delighted to see him fall for the lie. She was pleased by his frustration from his call being unanswered.

Juan called Cameisha's number repeatedly as he raced towards the house. He knew exactly where it was since he owned the property. Again and again, he got her voicemail. Since he wasn't the type to leave a message, he hung up and dialed again. The Dope Girl was in a deep sleep from getting dicked down by her Dope Boy.

"This is Meisha-Meisha, leave a name, and number so I can reach ya," she rapped on the recording.

Juan whipped into the driveway and proved his anti-lock brakes true, stopping an inch from the garage door. He hopped out and up the stairs in long angry strides.

Aqua heard the banging on the door, but had no intention on interrupting her shower. Her beloved was in a box under a tombstone, so she knew whoever it was wasn't there for her.

Samantha figured it wasn't for her either since she never invited anyone over. She was so frustrated over her scientific failure she tried to ignore the door. She easily flipped two kilos into eight but could not make it any stronger.

"Ok, ok," Samantha huffed when she saw that no one planned to get the door and the knocker was not giving up.

"Where is Cameisha?" Juan demanded as he stormed into the house. He scanned the empty living room before turning back to Samantha. He had yet to meet the talkative girl and was about to learn a lesson about asking her anything. Her crew had long ago stopped asking her questions. If they didn't know, they just wouldn't know.

Samantha took a deep breath...and went in!

"She's not here. I think she went to the apartment to take Self and Bad Ass somewhere. That nasty little boy has the right name, Bad Ass! Because he's a bad ass! He stared at my breasts the whole time and then whispered at me! You know what he said? I'll tell you what he said! Said he heard white girls give good head, but I don't know how true it is. They say all black guys have big dicks but all black guys don't have big dicks. Most dicks are normal but some are big, some are really big! I met this one guy..."

"Ok, ok!" Juan broke in waving his hands as if it would help stop the flow. "Where is Angela?"

"Angela?" Samantha answered the question with a question since they hadn't met. "No just me and Aqua. I spoke to Cameisha last night to tell her I couldn't make the cocaine any stronger. I think it may be dangerous too, I think Tommy may have OD'd..."

"Wait...you're the one who has been altering the cocaine?" Juan asked feeling his blood boil.

"Yup!" she sang proudly and got knocked the fuck out.

Juan hit her with a hard right that put her to sleep. He wasn't quite sure what was going on, but knew she was a vital part of it. He hoisted the sleeping girl onto his shoulder and carried her out to the car.

The trunk popped remotely as he neared and in went Samantha. Aqua had just reached her window in time to see Juan get behind the wheel. She shrugged it off and went to heat up one of her frozen Fat-Fat burgers.

"Manny, get everyone to the house. The whole family, now!" Juan barked into his phone when his brother answered. "We have a problem. A big fucking problem!"

"Everyone? Cameisha too?" Manny asked to clarify.

"No! Everyone except her. She's the problem!"

Chapter 2

Cameisha awoke snuggled up against Trigga. That morning like most mornings, she felt a nice stiff erection pressing against her ass. His heavy breathing resulted in a light snore signaling that he was still sleeping. That didn't stop Cameisha though. She was selfish like that. Meisha gets what Meisha wants, and if you planned to be a part of her world, you had to accept that.

She positioned the erection between her legs and grinded against it. It was enough to bust a nut, but she wasn't finished. She parted her wet lips in an effort to wriggle it inside her.

"You just gonna take the dick huh?" Trigga asked hoarsely.

"Shush and push," she instructed arching her back to help him inside her.

Trigga never like being told to shush or what to do, but since he was getting some pussy out of the deal, he shushed and pushed. Once he was safely inside, he lifted her leg so he could get a good stroke going. And what a good stroke it was, she came again a minute later. He wanted to beat it up since she got fly at the mouth, but couldn't last. Her moans and writhing in ecstasy pushed him over the edge. He bit down on her shoulder and exploded inside of her. Cameisha generously squeezed and grinded to get it all out.

"So, what's up for the day?" Meisha asked switching back to Dope Girl mode in an instant.

"Huh?" Trigga asked confused by the sudden switch. "Um, me and Troy gonna set up shop in Squeal n'dem 'partments."

"Y'all straight on work?"

"Yeah, for now. I'm finna lock the whole west side down so I'ma need more soon. A lot more," he said ambitiously.

"You lock down the west side 'cause the east side is mine!" she added as the conversation made its way to the shower. Seeing the place her Dope Boy daddy grew up and blew up in had her wide open.

9

Eastwyck Apartments was a fucking gold mine and she couldn't wait to dig in. The large apartment complex had a large population of addicts already and it was on busy Candler Road. I-20 ran alongside of it giving it easy access to traveling junkies. Suburban drug users could pull off the highway, cop, and return in just a few minutes.

The couple showered together yet separately with money on their minds. Once they washed the sex from their bodies, they stepped out and got dressed.

Meisha selected a pair of jeans tight enough to show off that fat ass yet loose enough to kick somebody in the mouth if somebody did or said something that warranted getting kicked in the mouth. She matched a cute top with some cute sneakers and packed a pistol into her purse.

Meanwhile, Trigga got dope boy fresh, just like a dope boy should. He pulled on an expensive pair of jeans and slung them low off his ass. His crispy white tee matched his crispy white tennis shoes and his hat matched his gat. He cocked the black Braves hat on his waves and tucked the polymer pistol in his pants.

Cameisha had to snap her head away from the sexy sight. Another second and she would have fucked him again and they wouldn't get anything done. Once they made it down to the garage, they traded a peck on the lips. They got into separate vehicles and went their separate ways. Now in business mode, they got down to business. As they pulled onto Peachtree, they both finally turned on their phones

"Dang," Meisha giggled as all the text, voicemails, emails, and social media notifications vibrated her phone for two minutes straight. She ignored them all and called her right hand man.

"Where you at yo!" Jackie barked when she took the call.

"I'm on my way to you. Get dressed," Cameisha replied.

"Get dressed? Girl, I been dressed! You acting like you ain't two hours late! I swear y'all young chicks be doing the most. I called Dasia, straight to voicemail. Called Samantha, straight to voicemail. Aqua talking 'bout she eating a Fat-Fat burger, call her back! You..."

"Was riding my man like a cowgirl," Cameisha giggled. "You must not have got you none last night. You all uptight."

"So! That ain't got nothing to do with it!" Jackie lied. That was exactly what was eating her since Ralphie was out of town instead of eating her. She clicked off and tossed her phone on the sofa beside her.

A few minutes later Cameisha made her presence known by blasting the car horn. She got a good giggle out of the perturbed look on Jackie's face as she came out.

"Y'all young broads," she reiterated even though she was only a couple of years older.

"Ain't none of them answering they phones 'cept Aqua and she still eating Fat-Fat burgers. Ma gon' have a fat-fat baby," Meisha laughed.

"So what you gotta show me?" Jackie asked reverting back to the animated conversation she started the day before. As soon as Trigga had walked in, she'd hung up in her face.

"That's where we going. Plus I gotta scoop these lil' niggas from there," she replied driving towards Decatur. When she spotted the Candler Road exit, she merged the Benz and got off. A couple of turns later, they were in the apartment complex. "Well?" Cameisha asked triumphantly as they cruised.

"Well what? Some projects?" she squawked. No sooner than she said it, did she start to get it. The drug trade was that obvious. She spotted Lil' Self and Bad Ass at the same time they spotted them.

When the youngins saw their ride, they turned to their little girlfriends and shoved their tongues into their mouths. They got last minute gropes and feels in before they parted.

"Get a room!" Meisha yelled from her window breaking up the long kiss goodbye.

"Cock blocker!" Bad Ass grumbled as he slid into the backseat. Self decided to use the same door and pushed him over. That set off another of their daily wrestling matches.

"Yo, I'm getting married," Lil' Self announced suddenly and seriously.

"Damn, that little black girl musta put it on your ass," Meisha said with a grimace.

"That's how us dark girls get down," Jackie co-signed. "The darker the berry the sweeter the juice!"

"I'm saying though...let a nigga sip the juice then," Bad Ass said seductively. Little nigga even licked his lips like LL Cool J hoping it might help his campaign.

"Shit I'll go to jail for fucking yo' little ass! Holla back when you get some hair on yo' face," Jackie laughed.

"Ask yo' girl Dasia how I rock," he shot back smugly.

"Speaking of D..." Cameisha mumbled and called her phone again. This time she got a different result that made her frown at her phone. Sure enough, it was Dasia's name and number on the screen but, "Her phone off?"

"Can't be, I just paid the bill on the phones," Jackie insisted. It was one of her duties so she took it personally.

"Anyway," Cameisha said nonchalantly but everyone felt the car speed up. "What you find out about the trap?"

"Yo, that shit booming ma! After I rocked my shorty to sleep, I went out to peep game. It's mad money out here!" Lil' Self exclaimed.

His little black girlfriend Angel had an older brother nicknamed Black who supplied the weight. Just ounces of cooked coke that the trap stars trap. Angel's mother demanded twenty out of him for spending the night. He sold enough dope in his short life to know full well what she was going to do with it and asked to inspect the product when she returned.

"Yo, that shit some garbage! Straight whip, dimes, and nicks," he explained.

"Sho-nuff?" Cameisha pondered aloud. The wheels in her head could be heard as they turned. There was no structure or order. Just a bunch of freelance dealers peddling for shoe and coochie money. "I need to holla at Black. Meanwhile y'all set up shop with that glass. Let's get these junkies to see things our way!"

Chapter 3

Trigga made it to the west side at the same time that Cameisha scooped up Self and Bad Ass. He frowned at the police activity in his apartment complex and kept right on driving. He caught a glimpse of Troy's car as he passed by.

"Let me see what's the deal," he muttered to himself as he pulled up to the corner store. He parked there and approached on foot. A sinking feeling hit him when he saw the official activity was at his mother's building.

Half of the building had been destroyed by fire. He slipped into the crowd of spectators who had gathered to gather information so they would have something to talk about later. Being on the scene allowed them to be the "they" in "they said." Think about it...

"What happened?" Trigga asked a large lady in a housecoat and rollers. The news reporter had already spotted her as their eyewitness.

"Miss Betty n'dem 'partment caught a fiyah!" she said proving she was the right pick to embarrass black folks. It was already out when she turned to see who she was speaking to. "I'm shole is sorry baby."

"Sorry for what..." Trigga began but was answered by the coroner. The body bag on the stretcher said all that needed saying.

"Hold up! Wait!" an officer yelled as Trigga ducked under the crime scene tape.

"Is that my momma?" he asked urgently.

"The deceased is believed to be Betty Jackson, but son, you don't want to see her like this," the officer said sympathetically. Trigga took his word for it, but still struggled out of frustration. That was what Troy arrived to see.

"What's up shawty?" Troy demanded ducking under the yellow tape and separating the two men.

"My momma..." Trigga croaked unable to get it all the way out. A single tear escaped his eye. It would be the only one.

"I know shawty, I know," he comforted and led him away.

Trigga knew he felt his pain since he recently lost his own mother. The only difference was this time there was no one to get revenge on. Even though the complex was teeming with police and other officials, Troy fired up a blunt as soon as they sat in his car. A cop frowned at the petty crime, but let it go.

"Pull 'round the corner to Oak Tree," Trigga announced after five minutes of mourning. Death is a part of life and the show must go on.

"Yeah it's time to put these niggas down with our lil' campaign," Troy agreed and put the car in gear.

Oak Tree Apartments was a virtual ghost town since the Salazar gunmen went through and sprayed the place. Now the dope boys were hungry and the crack heads were thirsty. Trigga was right on time. The trap stars got excited when they saw their savior coming to save them.

"What y'all got going on?" Trigga asked casually from shotgun. It was a rhetorical question since he knew they didn't have shit going on. They hadn't had any work since Squeal died.

"Shit. That's what we got going on. Jack shit!" DQ griped, twisting his lips.

"What Squeal was giving y'all off a G-pack?" Troy asked.

"A hunned!" Lil' Shock blurted truthfully and getting daggers shot at him by his friends who wanted room to negotiate. Both Trigga and Troy recognized him as their go to guy.

"Well, we pay two fiddy off one G-pack or..."

"Or same thing them Mexicans brought," Troy said picking up where Trigga left off. Sometimes a death threat can be a great negotiation tool. This was one of those times. All the dealers would much rather take $250 than get shot. And who could blame them?

"That's what's up!" DQ cheered and came forward with an empty palm.

Trigga tightened his finger on the trigger of the gun concealed under his shirt while Troy handed out the work. Five G-packs to the five trappers equaled a quick $3,750. That's good money while you're off making other money.

****

The roomful of Columbian killers was quiet and meek as they watched their boss pace back and forth. At the same time Juan tried to walk a hole in the carpet his brother worked the phones. Manny called everyone and anyone, looking for information on the missing woman. Finally, a return call delivered the news and it was not good.

"Si...si...adios mios!" Manny said crossing himself at the report. The action relayed the message to all except Juan.

"What? What!" he demanded, snatching his older and larger brother by his collar. "Que!"

"I'm sorry, she's gone," he said softly and took the abuse.

All the hearts in the room broke when Juan howled like a lady and collapsed. It was a very uncomfortable sight; seeing the boss cry like a bitch.

"Bring me the girl," he whimpered softly. No one moved because no one knew what he meant. Was he asking for his dead girlfriend or some other girl?

"What girl, hermano?" Manny finally asked.

"Blanca. The white girl. The one who talks a lot," he clarified. Manny snapped at Jose who rushed to carry out the command.

"Que pasa?" one of the family lieutenants inquired. "What is going on here Juan? Why are we here?"

"Cameisha...the black girl. She is the source of the tainted cocaine. She had the white girl alter it. She is the one who killed Angela. Mi madre said they argued on the phone and Angela went to see her," he explained.

"Cameisha killed Angela?" Manny exclaimed in disbelief. He wasn't the only skeptic. Dubious frowns spread amongst the uncles, cousins, and associates at the mention of Mama Salazar. Those who knew her well knew she was a lying snake. They also knew she was a very dangerous woman so they thought it but did not speak it.

"Por que?" Uncle Sosa asked. He witnessed how close they were. Heard him refer to her as his sister. "Why would she suddenly kill Angela? This makes no sense!"

"We're about to find out," Juan shot back firmly even though he wondered the same thing. None of it made any sense. Even Cameisha's hand in the poison drugs made no sense. Just then, Chaparo walked Samantha into the room. He wore the pained expression on his face of someone on the verge of being talked to death.

"You! Why did you sock me mister?" Samantha demanded when she saw Juan. Of course, she didn't wait for a response before launching into another one of her tirades.

"Chaparo grab the recorder. Manny, get Cameisha on the line," Juan ordered over the verbal assault. He walked over and pressed her mute button with another savage punch.

Chapter 4

"What?" Cameisha asked seeing Jackie's reaction when she hung up her phone. She already knew who she called.

"Now it's saying the number has been changed!" she growled. This was an 'I told you so' waiting to happen. Jackie didn't trust Dasia any further than she could throw her. She deceived the crew once so she couldn't understand why Cameisha trusted her again.

Cameisha didn't need to be reminded. She pressed on the gas and dipped in and out of traffic racing to the apartment.

"She prolly broke out with her girlfriend," Self snickered.

"I just can't see Dasia eating no pussy. I don't even eat no pussy!" Bad Ass announced, with his bad ass.

"And you tryna holla at me! Boy stop!" Jackie laughed.

"How 'bout you Self? You lick the candy jar?" Meisha asked via rearview mirror.

"Uh...um, no," Self lied. He subconsciously wiped his mouth cracking the occupants of the car up. The lighthearted banter paused the worry until they reached their destination.

Once they parked, Self had to run to stay ahead of Cameisha who was marching like a Korean soldier. He got the door open and stepped aside so she could enter.

"A-yo D! Where you at big face?" she called out playfully. She hoped the sleepy eyed girl would stagger out and explain away all their fears. However, it was not to be.

"A-yo Meish, look it!" Self called from the hallway. Cameisha rushed down and saw him frozen in place. He pointed at his kicked in door as if afraid to go further.

Cameisha didn't want to go in either so she went into Dasia's room instead. "Man..." she moaned at the empty room. Even though Dasia had a room at the house, she kept all clothes and shoes there and they were all gone. The suitcase they kept the weed in was the only thing left in the closet. Cameisha expected it to be bare, but to her surprise, it wasn't. A neat square equal to one fourth had been removed.

"Yo, we missing three bricks!" Self reported when Cameisha entered the boys' ransacked room. "We had 12."

"Why she leave nine?" Meisha pondered aloud.

"Well the bitch ain't leave no money. It was a buck and a half in here!" Jackie growled at the hundred and fifty thousand-dollar loss.

"A fourth! One fourth," Cameisha chuckled dryly as she figured it out. "She took her share."

"Her share! The bitch ain't got no share! If she wanted to bounce, she could bounce. She ain't entitled to no fourth of nothin'! And she took all the cash! I'ma kill that bitch!" Jackie screamed.

"No you're not," Meisha said calmly. "I'm going to kill her."

****

"This is it!" Lisa cheered and clapped as she pulled in front of a large Victorian home. It still showed a glimpse of its past glory with the ornate woodwork but it and the entire neighborhood had seen better days. "Come on!"

What the hell am I doing? Dasia asked herself for the hundredth time since fleeing Atlanta. She felt the regret of betraying her friend for some ass. The sight of Lisa's sweet ass rushing across the barren lawn provided some comfort.

"Look who's here!" Lisa announced through a raggedy screen door. She pulled it open and rushed inside, Dasia at her heels

"Oh!" Dasia grunted from the assault on her nostrils. The dim, dank, damp home smelled like old fish grease, malt liquor, shitty diapers, and the large lady smoking menthols.

"Is that my Li-Li?" the bearded lady screamed from her Lazy Boy chair. Hers should have been called a Lazy Lady chair because it's where the lazy lady spent most of her time.

The clutter around it provided everything she needed and the pickle jar full of pee served as her bathroom. She used her multitude of children and grandchildren as human remote controls to fetch what she needed. All day she barked orders like "Light Big Mama's cigarette. Roll Big Mama a blunt. Go play Big Mama's number and of course, change the TV."

"It's me," Lisa bounced and rushed over to hug her sweaty neck.

"Who yo' lil' friend?" Big Mama asked giving Dasia a once over as they hugged. Dasia wondered if she didn't like girls too.

"Oh this Dasia. Dasia this is Big Mama," she introduced backing away.

"Hey Big Mama," Dasia greeted with a handshake.

"Hey yo'self lil' mama," the old woman purred stroking Dasia's hand and proving her right. "Let Big Mama hold five dollars to play my numbers."

Everyone who has ever been used or taken advantage of can remember exactly when it started. They can vividly recall the first yes that caused the trickle that broke the dam and flooded the town. The yes that should have been a resounding no! A hell no, fuck outta here.

"Um...sure," Dasia agreed and went for her purse. Time stopped in the rundown house when cash came into view.

Big Mama wished she had asked for more when she saw the roll. A snotty nose baby boy with a sagging diaper walked over and stuck out his dirty hand. The toddler toddled her for some cash too. The naked little girl saw the money and started dancing. Just like her ratchet mother did in the strip club every night.

"Do I smell money?" a slimy little man asked as he slithered around a corner. The dope fiend could actually smell money. He may have never worked a day in his life, but he could suck coins out of a vending machine. Or hold his breath for five minutes collecting change from fountains and wishing wells.

"Un uh Uncle Mark!" Lisa shouted but it was too late. He'd already seen the money.

"Hey lil' mama, I'm yo' uncle Mark," he said as he enveloped Dasia in a funky hug.

"Oh!" Dasia gasped and held her breath as the smell from his underarms and funky balls wafted into her life.

"So good to see you again," he said rocking with her like they were old friends. It wasn't until Dasia felt his dope fiend dick getting hard that she push away.

"Here you go Big Mama," she said peeling off a ten instead of the five. That's called adding fuel to the fire.

"Let me hold a hunned!" Mark asked trying his luck.

"Ain't nobody giving you no damn hundred dollars!" Lisa shouted in her own defense.

"A'ight, a'ight five then. Jelly n'dem got fat balloons of that diesel for five," he announced causing Lisa to flinch. Dasia saw the odd reaction but didn't understand it. Not yet, anyway, but she would.

"Sure," Dasia agreed and gave him a five. The cool baby came over and she gave him a one. The future THOT got a bill too and started dancing.

"Y'all ate yet? Y'all want some of Big Mama's fried chicken, macaroni and cheese, candy yams, and collards," she enticed.

"Hell yeah!" Lisa shouted with Dasia nodding beside her.

The girls had just come off a three-day coke binge of no food or sleep. They ate a lot of pussy and eating pussy may be rewarding and fulfilling but it's not very filling. Man cannot live on vagina alone. Neither can women.

"Ok, y'all go to the sto' and grab some chicken, macaroni, cheese, collards, and sweet potatoes. Oh and a 40 of malt liquor and play 5-6-9 box, straight, and twist," Big Mama said tucking the ten under one of her big ass titties. No telling what all was under those things.

Uncle Mark caught a ride to the store with the girls. When they went inside to shop, he bent a corner to cop. Big Mama's final list filled up an entire shopping cart. Lisa walked away from the register when the three hundred dollar total appeared.

They got back to the car just as Mark finished cooking his dope. Just in time to see him push the plunger sending the heroin into his veins. He passed gas loudly and went into a nod. Lisa felt her panties get wet remembering what that felt like. Her addiction ran her to Atlanta, but now she was home.

Dasia ignored the smell, the roaches, and the big ass stain in Big Mama's nightshirt that she wore all day every day. Despite the nastiness, the food was delicious. She even pretended not to see the ashes that fell into the collards and ate them too.

"That was great Big Mama," she sang appreciatively.

"Thank you child. Where y'all staying Li-Li?" Big Mama asked.

"We gon' get a hotel until we find an apartment..."

"No such a thing! Y'all gon' stay rat here until you find a place," the woman insisted. She evicted Mark from his room to make space.

The food, long drive, and lack of sleep left Dasia too tired to argue. She followed Lisa up to Mark's heroin paraphernalia cluttered room. Burnt bottle tops, matches, and used syringes littered the cramped room. The bed had the dirty imprint of a man on the dirty sheet. Dasia was too tired to argue so she climbed on, fully dressed, and passed out. Luckily, for her, she put her cash filled purse under her body as she slept. The bulk of the money was stashed in her suitcase in the car.

Dasia smelled Mark enter the room but pretended to sleep. She felt him standing over her and peeked out from under a clenched eyelid. There was Unc staring at her crotch and pulling on his dope fiend dick. She felt a glob of semen hit her leg when he came with a grunt. When they awoke the next morning, she insisted on a hotel.

Chapter 5

"Let's see if you're ready to talk now chica!" Juan said smugly once he got word that everyone was in place. His previous calls had all gone to voicemail. He stuck his chest out since he had an audience and put the call on speakerphone. "I have..."

"Yo Juan, I can't talk right now. I got a situation!" Cameisha blurted and hung up. Some of the stolen money belonged to him for what he fronted her as well as the next re-up. She would have to flip the remaining drugs just to break even. "Any word from Sam?"

"Still voicemail," Jackie said twisting her lips in thought.

"I...huh?" Juan asked the dead phone. He snapped his finger at the thought that popped in his head. He took a picture of the girl asleep at his feet and texted it to Cameisha. Then he crossed his arms and waited for the call he knew was coming.

"Well, Dasia's mom ain't heard from her either," Meisha frowned when she hung up from the call to New York. She knew it was a long shot since Dasia walked away from her mother and son and never looked back.

Cameisha was about to catch an attitude when a text from Juan vibrated her phone. She frowned seeing it was a picture message, something he never did. She wondered again for the hundredth time, what his dick looked like and quickly opened the picture.

"What?" Jackie screamed matching the look of terror on her race. Cameisha dropped the phone and backed away from holding her hands to her face like she was "Home Alone." She was too shocked for words so Jackie picked up the phone to see for herself. "Samantha? Is she...dead? What's going on Meisha?"

"I don't know but I'm 'bout to find out!" she growled snapping out of it. She snatched the phone and dialed Juan on the speakerphone.

"Still too busy to talk?" Juan asked smugly after letting it ring several times before picking up. The hint of sass in his voice made Jackie picture him with his hand on a hip and rolling his neck.

"Did you kill my friend?" Meisha moaned.

"Did you kill my woman?" he shot back.

"Huh? What the hell are you talking about? I haven't seen Angela in..."

"Lies!" Juan shouted loud enough to wake Samantha from her right hook induced nap. "You and her argued last night. She went to see you and never came home. Her body was found this morning! My mother heard you arguing with her!"

"Hey! Why did you hit me? A guy hit me like that once before because..." Samantha yelled to Cameisha and Jackie's relief. It was short lived though.

"Listen, Juan, I don't know what's going on but..."

"What about the cocaine? Don't know about that either? Your friend here says otherwise. You betrayed me! Qisas, an eye for an eye!" he cut in.

"Wait! Please wait," Meisha pleaded. "Let me come explain."

"Ok. Just stay right there. I'm on my way but say goodbye to your friend," Juan said calmly.

"He...hello," Samantha said when he pushed the phone in front of her.

"Don't worry Sam, I..." was all Cameisha was able to get out before a loud gunshot rang out and the line went dead.

"He killed her," Meisha moaned and sank slowly to the floor. Her friend was dead because of her and she knew it. Jackie was devastated as well, but knew that wasn't the time for mourning. She caught the threat in Juan's statement and got in motion.

"Self, grab the coke. Bad Ass get the weed and whatever else y'all keeping!" she instructed then turned to Cameisha. "Up, up, come on. Get up! We gotta go. Now!"

Cameisha moved lethargically as Jackie led her out to the car. Self and Bad Ass hoped in the backseat seconds before Jackie pulled off. A gut feeling told her to bust a left instead of a right so she did. Just as she hit one corner, a carload of stern faced Columbians hit the other. They missed each other by seconds.

The car pulled to a screeching stop in front of the building and they rushed inside with guns drawn. The lead man didn't even slow down when they reached the door. Instead, he lowered his shoulder and ran straight through it. The gunmen fanned out searching each room like a drug task force. And just like the police, they planned to murder anything moving.

"Aqua!" Cameisha suddenly realized. If Juan were coming at her, he would check there as well. She whipped out her phone and called her friend. "Pick up, pick up, pick up!"

"Hello?" Aqua mumbled with a mouthful of Fat-Fat burger.

"Aqua? Get the work from Samantha's room and get out of there now!" she shouted urgently.

"Modqri?"

"Now Aqua now! Grab the blow and get out!" Meisha yelled while Jackie stomped on the gas pedal. She whipped in and out of traffic like a Manhattan cab driver.

Aqua was a little slow, but knew danger when she heard it. She didn't know what was going on and didn't need to. Her first guess was police so the four kilos of cocaine were top priority. She rushed into Samantha's lab/room and scooped up the bricks. The new mouse stole her attention momentarily. He was in his little wheel running his little ass off.

"Oh!" she said remembering her Fat-Fat burgers in the freezer. Once she retrieved them, she hit the door. No sooner did she step away from the house a large brown truck pulled on to the street. The men all stared at Aqua as they passed her. She didn't fit the description so they pushed on.

The truck backed in front of the house and opened the roll up door. Inside a Vulcan 20mm Gatling gun was mounted on a heavy-duty tripod. All of the occupants pulled ear protectors on their ears knowing what was to come.

"Brr, brr, brr," the six-barrel machine gun belched as it sent 100 rounds a second into the house. The ammo drum emptied in seconds and was quickly replaced by another. Another, and then another.

The Columbian man manning the cannon took his sweet time as he methodically sprayed the house with the huge slugs. He used slow, even strokes to ensure each inch was shot the fuck up. Windows and walls broke and buckled under the pressure. A bright orange fire proved the gas line had been ruptured. Their job was done so the door came down and they pulled away.

Aqua stepped as quickly as she could pretending not to hear the roar of the machine gun. She didn't even flinch at the sound of the explosion behind her. The truck slowed when they reached her. A passenger extended a pistol and aimed it at the back of her head. He began to slowly squeeze the trigger until stopped by a downward glance.

"Adios mio," he said pulling the gun in at the sight of her baby bump. Most of it was Fat-Fat burgers, but it saved her life. He crossed himself religiously as they pulled off.

Aqua marched casually munching on a frozen Fat-Fat burger as if she didn't see her near murder. The girl had more balls than a lot of men. Still, once the truck was gone she collapsed on the sidewalk. That's exactly where Cameisha and company found her when they arrived.

"A-yo, who the fuck is this nigga you beefing with?" Lil' Self exclaimed when they drove past the demolished house.

"Nobody," Cameisha barked defiantly even though she knew she was in trouble. In over her head with more than she could handle. Yeah, she was a killer with an uncle named Killa, but she was out of her league. Common sense told her to get on the highway and drive west until she reached the ocean. But when did Cameisha ever follow common sense?

Chapter 6

"Juan Salazar, age 30. Defacto head of the Salazar drug empire. Brother Manuel is five years his senior but mentally ten years his junior. He is the brawn to his brain. Marisol Salazar is the matriarch and she's one dangerous bitch. She was suspected in a slew of murders in Columbia, some against her own family members. Somehow both she and the charges vanished, and she pops up here with a clean slate," Detective Walton briefed.

He pointed a laser pointer at the pyramid of pictures on the wall behind him. He relayed the latest intel on all of the players until he got down to the last picture on the bottom. This was the one piece of the puzzle that puzzled him. It was in the box with all the other pieces yet it just didn't seem to fit.

"Just how does the girl fit in?" a rookie named Brice asked when no info came on her. All heads in attendance snapped in his direction at the breach in protocol. Walton had a rule they all lived by. Shut the fuck up during briefings. Since he was new, he received his first and only pass. Repeat violators of the S.T.F.U rule found themselves back in uniform.

Brice hadn't taken his eyes off the pretty, young girl for more than a few seconds at a time since the briefing began. He paid close attention and could replay every word if need be, but something about the girl got to him.

At 6'1", 190 pounds, with caramel skin the 22 year old was a pretty young thing himself. The south side Atlanta native had made some good choices in his short life. He had chosen to work part-time in a supermarket while most of his friends sold drugs. He had chosen to graduate on time rather than drop out. Again, he won when he picked college over prison. The police force would be stable employment with good benefits while pursuing a law degree. His eyes were focused on the Supreme Court as the final prize.

After completing the police academy, he was quickly recruited by the drug task force. Walton personally picked him by looks alone, but he was also very qualified. Dress him in the latest fashions and he'd fit right in the underworld.

"I'm not quite sure," Agent Marks spoke up. He personally trailed her from the meeting with the Salazars and came up with nothing. "Typical girl stuff consisting of hair, nails, and Chipotle. Later that night they turned up in a trendy club and 'Turnt up.'"

"And I don't buy it," the veteran cop barked. "She was at an upper echelon meeting with the largest cocaine ring in the city! And of course our very own Anna Flores was there too."

All eyes turned to the picture of Anna. Even though she worked in the Medical Examiner's office, she was sill supposed to be on their team. One of the good guys, but there she was hobnobbing with the bad guys.

"What's the deal with her?" Toshiba Watkins asked scrunching up her pretty face. The thirty-year-old woman was a ten-year veteran of the Atlanta police department.

"Nothing, a fucking waitress. She feeds information to the clan but we'll be cooking the food. We can control what they get," Walton replied since it was now the question and answer part of the briefing.

"What ever happened to the doctor? The one she was dating, the pill guy?" Marks inquired.

Brice listened intently to the information on a boyfriend with a tinge of jealousy. Again, the veteran cop caught his interest in the girl and smiled internally. He wanted him to take interest in her. Planned on it actually.

"A patsy, a sap, a real sucker. He was squeaky clean and took the rap for her. Now he's serving time for it," Walton relayed.

"But why? Why go through all that? Why lose everything?" Brice asked with a pained expression.

Again, all heads snapped in his direction at the inane questions. Toshiba smiled warmly at his innocent naiveté. It was refreshing to see a youth uncorrupted by the ways of the word. Dangerous, but refreshing.

Detective Walton smiled too, for the same reason. He came over sat on his desk, and gently explained. "Son, have you ever had some really, really...good pussy?"

****

Bilal didn't get much time since he didn't have much of a case. He was sent to a comfy federal prison camp that looked more like a college campus than a jail. Of course, he decided to be an author like everybody else who goes to jail. It should have been and would have been an easy bid if not for his brother. Every day that Bilal refused to join him, he turned up the pressure. Pressure busts pipes you know.

"Yo' brudda on da phone," Mo announced as he barged into Bilal's cell without knocking.

That was a sign of disrespect, but that was the point. Technically cell phones are illegal contraband but money moves mountains. With the right amount of cash to spread around an inmate can have all the comforts of home. Wine, women, weed, whatever could be bought or sold. Suave had the bread to spread, but his little brother wanted no parts of it.

"Tell him I don't want to speak with him," Bilal said rolling his eyes. The epicene move made Mo's dick jump, with his gay ass.

"Tell me yourself, you little bitch," Suave said confirming that the call was on speaker. "That's exactly what you sound like. Exactly what you acting like, a bitch!"

"What...ever!" Bilal said making Mo rock hard. A large erection poked straight out in his sweat pants.

"The whatever is you gon' do what I told you to do! The second you come home. If you get released on a Monday and that bitch is dead by Tuesday!"

"You leave Cameisha alone!" he yelled directly into the phone. Mo moved it down a little so it would be closer to his dick. "You touch her and I'll..."

"You'll what? Cry? Call the cops? You a snitch too now? 'Sides I'm not going to touch her, you are. Please don't think you can't get touched in there. Mo, tell him he can get touched in there."

"Mm hm, shole can," Mo said licking his lips at Bilal. He even gave the lump in his pants a stroke so there would be no misunderstanding. "Fuck around and get fucked around."

Bilal stumbled away from the big man and his big lump. He didn't want to get fucked at all and especially by that. The call ended but Mo stood there surveying him up and down. He looked at him the way a man does a woman, or the way a man who likes men does a man he likes. Mo liked men.

****

"So what do we do with her?" Manny asked looking down at Samantha balled in a fetal position, but breathing.

"Take her to the green house. She will show us how she alters the cocaine. Won't you?" Juan demanded.

"Y...y...yes," she replied taking the first breath since Juan fired a shot into the ceiling. She opened her mouth to speak again, but a sharp pain reminded her of what happened last time she spoke. For the first time since she was three, she settled for a one-word answer.

The Salazar clan owned real estate all over Atlanta and the surrounding counties. Some were legit rental properties while others housed family and associates. A series of stash and safe houses were also maintained. They were referred to by color rather than location.

The white house was the one out in Gwinnet County that he let Cameisha and company use. It was now a smoldering ruin thanks to the Gatling gun. The brown house down south in Henry County was used to process the cash. It held millions in drug money on a regular basis.

The green house was a gated estate in Vinings. It was pretty plush for a prison and where Samantha would be held.

"Juan?" Manny began once the room was cleared. "If the altered cocaine is killing people, why are we making it?"

"Killing who? Exactly who is dying from the drugs?" he shot back. The way he tilted his head proved a point was forthcoming after the answer.

"Drug users, addicts?" his brother answered unsurely.

"Black, drug users and addicts! And the police think it was from the black dealers. We'll make the money and let them sort it out!"

Chapter 7

The sight of how badly the white house was shot up consumed everyone's thoughts as they rode back towards the city. Meisha was more angry than sad about Samantha's presumed murder. Sure, it was her fault, but the way her selfishness was set up it wouldn't allow her to acknowledge it. Jackie knew it too, but the way her loyalty was set up she didn't do 'I told you so's.'

"At least no one knows where this place is," Cameisha sighed when she pulled into the condo unit's underground parking. She and Trigga had a pact that absolutely no one knew where they laid their heads at night. It was a good rule to have.

"Fo' real though," Jackie said with a sting in her voice. She understood it, but knew she was as trustworthy as they came. Her friend heard it, but let it pass. It was a moot issue now that they were there.

"Yo, this shit is ill!" Bad Ass shouted when Meisha opened the door and stepped aside so they could enter. He rushed over to the floor to ceiling windows that overlooked the city and looked over the city.

"This is nice!" Jackie co-signed as she stepped onto the hardwood flooring. A tan leather sofa and loveseat contrasted quite nicely against the dark wood.

"Where's the microwave?" Aqua wanted to know. She had no intention on eating another frozen Fat-Fat burger. A glance around the condo answered the question for her when she spotted it. She stuck two burgers in and hit the button. Next, she hit the stainless steel fridge in search of something to wash it down with.

"Yo! It's only one bedroom!" Lil Self called from the one bedroom. He came back up front and asked, "Where we 'posed to sleep?"

"Well I stay with my man so y'all can't come there," Jackie threw out before anyone asked.

"Don't act like y'all niggas ain't never slept on no floor! It'll only be for a second until we figure something out," Cameisha replied.

"Trigga won't mind?" Aqua asked with Fat-Fat juice running down her chin.

"He won't...we 'bout to see," Cameisha started, stopped, and continued when in walked Trigga. "Hey bae! ...What's wrong?"

"My momma died...what's going on?" he replied. A frown of curiosity crossed his face at the room full of people. The broken rule could only mean disaster struck.

"Oh, my God! I'm so sorry!" Aqua wailed, rushed over, and snatched him into a bear hug. Fat-Fat grease, sauce, and cheese smeared against his face while all the air was forced from his lean body.

"I uh..." was all he could get out. Luckily, Cameisha had been hugged by Aqua before and knew what he was going through.

"I'm sorry bae, Aqua let him go so we can talk," she said saving him from passing out.

Trigga sucked in a gulp of air when he was released then followed his girl into the bedroom. He closed the door behind him and sat down. Cameisha paced for a second trying to figure out how to best spin the story. Another life was lost because of her bullshit but she was too immature to admit or accept that.

"Samantha's dead. Juan killed her. Tried to kill me too but...where you going?" she asked when Trigga jumped up and headed for the door.

"Finna go murk that nigga," he replied as if it were just that simple. Just walk up to Juan Salazar and shoot him. The President would be easier to touch now that the Columbians had circled the wagons.

"Bae, he's out of our league. You gotta see what they did to the house. I think he got a Black Hawk helicopter or something." That was enough to sit Trigga back down.

"Why? Why would he kill your girl? Why would he try to kill you? I know the money straight, you ain't snitch, so why?" He had to know.

"He claims I killed his girl last night."

"Last night? Only thing got kilt last night was that coochie!" he shot back proudly. Men take pride when they know they beat it up properly. The way he put it down there was no question. Meisha curled up like a baby with her thumb in her mouth and passed out once they finished. Then practically raped him in the morning.

"You did yo' thing baby!" Cameisha admitted jovially then got back to the business at hand. "He claims his mother said me and her argued and she came to see me."

"What y'all was beefing about?" Trigga asked.

"Nothing! That bitch is lying! It don't even matter now. He killed my girl and I'm going to kill him for it. His lying ass mother too!"

"Ok, so what we gon' do after you kill the connect? I just moved into another apartment complex. I'm finna sew up the whole west side," Trigga announced, switching back to dope boy mode.

"Sew it up then cuz the east side is mine! I just came across a gold mine. Once I lock Eastwyck down, the city gotta come on in! And I ain't selling no weight, you wanna trap, trap for me," she greedily agreed. She of all people should know better than to try and stop other people from eating. She had put a slug in Munch's ass up in the Bronx for the exact same thing.

"Only...you fucked up the connect," he reminded

"So! He ain't the only nigga in the city with 100% pure Columbian cocaine for the low! ...Yes he is...Fuck we gon' do now?" Meisha moaned.

"I got a brick left. The way Oak Tree be popping that ain't gon' last but a minute."

"I got 12...no 13, so we good for a week or two. I'ma let the shorties test the waters tomorrow in Eastwyck. Once that catch it'll burn through a brick a day," Meisha surmised.

"What you gon' do 'bout them?" Trigga asked. "Aqua can sleep in here with you and I'll hang out with them lil' dudes."

"Just for the night!" Meisha shouted. She was thinking with her vagina and wanted her own personal plumber lying next to her at night.

"Real talk, I gotta find a spot to get my girl out of the line of fire. Gotta set up shop in Eastwyck too."

"I gotta give it to you shawty. You're a Dope Girl fo' real!"

Chapter 8

"Man this is not what I bought these expensive ass pots for!" Cameisha grumbled as she worked. Cooking up all that cocaine was a lot of work indeed. When she pulled her surgical mask over her mouth and nose, Trigga and Self did the same. Bad Ass just leaned in with his mask still around his neck.

"May as well get you a shooter and take a blast shawty," Trigga warned muffled from under his mask.

"Huh?" Bad Ass shot back reeling from the disgusting notion. A crack pipe cost him both his parents and put him on the streets. No way would he ever use the dangerous drug.

"He right. You keep breathing these fumes and yo' lil' ass gon' be strung out," Cameisha co-signed. That was why so many dealers ended up being users. They go from tipping the doorman to being the doorman.

"Oh!" he said and covered his mouth and nose like everyone else.

The kitchen was thrust into complete silence as the three dope boys watched the dope girl work her magic. The only sound to be heard was Aqua laughing at cartoons in the next room.

Beef or no beef, Cameisha didn't plan to give the streets a break. Even without a connect; she had to get her money. The plan was to cook and sell all the remaining coke retail. That was an easy half a million dollars but still not enough for the greedy girl. She searched her memory bank while she worked for a replacement supplier. Cameisha cooked four ounces at a time and the finished product was pure butter.

"Damn shawty, this shit gon' knock they socks off!" Trigga grimaced. They had been talking shit about who was the best dope cooker all night. They agreed to a cook off, but Trigga just conceded after the first batch. "You got that."

"I know I got that!" the cocky girl boasted and popped her invisible collar. "Now y'all niggas get to choppin'!"

37

Every time a batch was cooked and dried, it was transferred to the long glass table in the dining room. The boys had set up an assembly line for the product. Lil Self cut nicks for the Eastwyck trade and Bad Ass stuffed them into tiny blue bags.

Trigga kept his remaining kilo separate. He cut it into ten-dollar increments, and then combined the thousand-dollar bomb known as G-packs. Each one represented seven hundred and fifty dollars after paying the trappers. He would end up with 70 of them for a total of over fifty thousand dollars. He intended to flip his as soon as possible and get more before they were all gone.

"Say shawty, I'ma hit you with the first 36 I brang in and cop two more of them thangs!" Trigga called into the kitchen.

"They twenty bands now. We at the bottom of the barrel," she called back not even turning in his direction. Both Self and Bad Ass's eyes grew wide as she instantly raised the price on her own man. They didn't understand, but he did.

"Dope Girl fo' real!" Trigga laughed heartily. He immediately began cutting the dimes a hair smaller to absorb the price increase. Dude was a dope boy for real. The law of supply and demand applies to all industries including selling dope. Once Trigga's kilo was cooked and cut, it was time to hit the trap. He alerted Troy to meet him at the apartments.

****

"That's fucked up shawty! What we 'posed to do now? Ain't nobody got no good dope in the city 'cept the Mexicans!" Troy lamented when Trigga relayed the news of the lost connect.

"My girl working on it. Shit she from New Yawk, you know they got that work up there. They got all kinda Mexicans from all over," Trigga replied proving he wasn't much on geography.

"This shit look different!" Troy declared when Trigga showed him the product. He stuck his nose in the bag and pulled away with a happy frown. "This that butter! Straight glass! Pure..."

"Ok, ok, it's straight," he said twisting his lips. Cameisha won the cook off, no need to rub it in. "That Oak Tree money was straight?"

"Every cent! Them niggas is on point," he answered. Lil Shock and company brought back $750 on each G-pack just like they should have. It was all good money too, fifties, twenties, even a few c-notes and tens."

Any time a trapper pays with a bunch of ones and fives it means he struggled to get it up. He was a problem waiting to happen. You might as well shoot him then and save a couple bucks.

"Let's hit Oak Tree off first," Troy suggested oddly since they were already in Westfield.

Trigga knew his friend long enough to smell an ulterior motive. He shrugged his shoulders in agreement so he could see what it was. He had a feeling and he was right.

Every ghetto apartment complex in the world has its own dope boys. Any time you have dope boys you have hoes that love them. That shit goes together like peanut butter and jelly. Generally, dudes from other spots didn't mess with the local hoes. They were too much trouble, and might set you up to get robbed or murdered. Better to stick to your own hoes, safer. But now that Troy and Trigga were supplying the dope boys, they had access to their hoes. It's in the rulebook. To the victor goes the spoils. Booty.

Once they pulled into Oak Tree, Trigga pulled his pistol and laid it on the center console. Guns might not talk but they do speak for themselves. Troy arrived at the track lighting up the faces of the dope boys.

"Sup shawty," he greeted as his window slid down.

"You tell me!" DQ said excitedly. He nodded a 'what's up' to Trigga and the pistol, but neither said anything in reply. Nonetheless, he along with the other trappers, were happy to see the men. Without a steady flow of dope, the dope boys were broke. If they were broke then the hoes were broke. The only thing worse than a broke dope boy is a broke hoe.

"Same as before," Troy said and began handing out the G-packs. The ten workers represented 7,500 bucks while they were off doing other things. Both had other things to do.

Trigga had to go downtown to formally identify his mother. That would set the funeral process in motion. The fire had started the job, but Ms. Jackson would still have to be cremated.

Still, it was better than how his brother Keith made out. Since no one claimed him, he was still in the morgue a few drawers down from his mother. Eventually, he would end up buried in a pulpwood box in a potter's field. A plain marker reading John Doe number something would be on the grave. A fitting burial for the piece of shit that he was. America should build a big ass toilet so they could just flush people like him.

Troy had something to do too, and she was headed his way.

"Hey Trigga, hey Troy," Nita-Boo sang as she switched her fine yellow ass towards them.

No one would ever accuse Nita-Boo of being pretty, but she was a fine motherfucker. She had a beautiful mulatto skin tone and long sandy brown hair. Her full lips had a purple hue to them due to menthol and blunt smoking. She had her short shorts pulled into her crotch so no one would have to wonder if her vagina was fat or not. It clearly was. The other hoes fell in behind her since she was the head hoe in charge. The spokes-hoe.

"Sup," was all they got out of Trigga who turned away to prove he was not interested. Nita-Boo knew he was the boss so she tried him first. She registered the snub and turned her sights on Troy.

"Sup with you then Troy?" she asked making sure to show off her tongue ring. She lolled out her tongue and licked her purple lips. It was body language for 'I'll suck your dick right here.'

"Shit, I'm tryna cut something. You then her, her, and her," he said laying out his plans to run through the crew.

"That's what's up," Nita-Boo agreed while her hoes nodded behind her. They all fucked the same dudes anyway. All of their children were somehow related. Except for Nita-Boo who didn't have any. She had plenty of abortions, but no children.

"Get ready. I'm finna drop my people off and fall through," Troy ordered and pulled away without waiting for a reply. It's not like she was going to say no, she's a hoe.

"So you ain't tryna fuck nothing but yo' ol' lady huh?" Troy asked as they left the apartment complex.

"For what? I got a good woman at home, why would I fuck around?" Trigga replied with the million-dollar question. No one can answer it because it just doesn't make sense.

The drive back over to their apartment complex was quiet as they contemplated what was next. After breaking off ten more G-packs to ten more trappers, they went their separate ways.

****

Trigga had been so deep in thought that he drove as if on autopilot. He was so familiar with the Atlanta streets that he made the turns without thinking about them. Before he knew it, he was at the morgue. He deliberately drove a few extra blocks so he could walk back and get his mind right. After showing his ID, he had a brief wait until someone came to escort him to the rear.

"Mr. Jackson? I'm Anna Flores," she introduced herself with a warm smile and handshake. Neither had any idea that they were on opposite sides of the war that was brewing.

"Hey," Trigga greeted stoically and looked down. Anna had a thing for black men but never acted on it due to the powerful clan she belonged to. Still, she admired the handsome thug in front of her.

"Due to the extent of damage from the fire we can't actually show you the body," Anna offered as she led him to the rear. "We've already verified her identity so you'll just have to sign and arrange for burial."

"My momma burned to death?" Trigga lamented as the full weight of it landed on his shoulders. Anna hated to break protocol but felt his pain.

"No, there was no smoke in her lungs. She had a heart attack and died before the fire could kill her," she admitted. Of course, she left out the fact that his mother was added to the list of people who had died from bad Salazar dope. A problem that should have been fixed when tiny pieces of Squeal came through her office.

"Oh, ok," he said feeling a little better. "Guess I'll call Clayton and Sons to pick her up."

"Ok...if you need anything else...give me a call," Anna said surprising herself and passing her card. The tone was very personal and Trigga heard it.

"What you Mexican or something?" he asked surprising himself when he accepted it.

"No, not all Hispanics are Mexican!" she giggled. "I'm Columbian."

"Columbian!" he cheered. Trigga might not know much about geography, but he knew Columbia was where the best cocaine came from.

****

When Trigga pulled out Troy was right behind him. Instead of left, he turned right and headed back to Oak Tree. Trigga laughed knowingly when he saw him in his rearview mirror. He could only hope the boy had some condoms because he was sure the girl had a petri dish in her panties.

"Here go my ride bitches," Nita-Boo announced triumphantly when she saw Troy pull in. She had won first place in the dope boy sweepstakes. Sure, he was going to fuck all her friends, but she was first.

She hopped off the hood of the hooptie they were perched on and tugged her shorts back up into her crotch.

"Put it on him girl," Ta-Ta cheered. She was second on the hoe-tum pole and would fuck him next. Shay-Shay and Meeka would follow.

Troy pulled over and popped the locks so she could get it. Once her round cheeks hit the leather he hit the gas and passed her a smoldering blunt. "What you drankin' shawty?"

"Boy you know I fucks with that Real Nigga 9000!" she cheered.

Real Nigga 9000 was the latest high alcohol content concoction manufactured and marketed to inner city blacks. It only came in big 60-ounce bottles to make sure you're good and fucked up. The neck of the bottle was made like a handle to make sure you could fuck somebody up with it.

Even though it was produced by a white supremacy group, they hired a popular rapper to push their poison. A dumb ass rapper who went by the name Verb got the call. He put it in a song and video and sales skyrocketed. The group produced Trailer Park Potion for poor whites and Tonto 2000 for the reservations. All they had to do then was sit back and watch the news.

Troy pulled out of the complex then pulled over at the corner store. He peeled a five from the inside of a large roll of cash and sent her inside for her drank. When she returned he bent a few corners and stopped at the local fuck hotel.

The one star motel was very rarely slept in. Most people went to either fuck or smoke crack. No one would actually sleep with the class of female that would let you fuck her in there and crack heads never sleep. They stay wide-awake stealing, smoking and burning bridges until they die.

Since it was established that they were there to fuck, the couple began undressing as soon as they walked into the musty room. Undressing is actually foreplay and Nita-Boo knew it. The pro-hoe had worked enough strip clubs to know how to make undressing an adventure. And she didn't have many clothes on to begin with.

Troy unbuckled his belt and let the heavy jeans fall to the floor. He stepped out of them while pulling his shirt over his head. He climbed atop the sweat, cum, blood, beer stained comforter and lit another blunt to watch the show.

Nita-Boo guzzled 20 of the 60 ounces and sat the bottle down. She slowly lifted her shirt over her head and unfastened her bra. When the big yellow breasts capped with wide brown nipples came out Troy felt his erection begin to rise. She turned around and bent over to remove her cheap sandals. When she came back up, she peeled the tiny shorts along with her panties off in one movement. Troy smiled at the pleasantly plump, shaved vagina.

He held out the blunt as she joined him on the bed. She took a heavy pull from between his fingers and got to work. Nita-Boo made his whole dick disappear into her mouth while smoke billowed from his nostrils, and that was some sexy shit. She worked her lips, tongue, head, and tonsils in magical harmony. A few minutes later, she was sucking cum from his dick like a milkshake. She kept right on sucking too; to make sure he stayed hard. He did so she came up and prepared to mount him backward.

"Hold up shawty! Put some rubber on that wood. Grab them out my pocket. My back pocket," he specified to keep her away from the cash in the front pocket.

Troy got another show when she bent over to retrieve the lifesaving latex. Not lifesaving as in she had AIDS but as in, if she got pregnant she would kill it. She had so many abortions she should get a tattooed tear under her eye like other killers do.

Nita-Boo was really putting on when she put the condom on with her mouth. She let it touch her tonsils once more then put him inside her and rode him backwards. She made sure to lean forward so he could see every slow, squishy wet stroke. When she started making circles with her yellow ass, he grabbed his phone to record it just like he was supposed to. The freak show would have went on all day if not for text messages coming in from both complexes.

"Damn the trap poppin'!" he exclaimed seeing trapper after trapper's urgent plea for more dope. "We gotta bounce!"

He flipped her over on her back, scooped her legs onto his shoulders, and pounded. Luckily, she got another nut before he did because the second he did, he pulled out and got up. They quickly got dressed and rushed out to the car.

"Put this in your pocket," Troy said handing Nita-Boo a hundred dollar bill. See it's only tricking if you pay before you fuck. Pay afterwards and it's just breaking bread. He made his rounds and collected 15k, then passed out another twenty G-packs. Today was going to be a good day.

Chapter 9

"A-yo, y'all lil' niggas go slow. Don't step on no toes. Just feel the shit out, feel me?" Cameisha coached as she drove Self and Bad Ass out to Eastwyck. She gave them each half a G-pack to test the waters. She had repeated it three times already to make sure it sank in. It didn't.

"Go slow? I'ma go hard! Yo we 'bout to eat out that bitch!" Bad Ass shouted from the backseat. Self just shook his head knowing Cameisha was about to snap. She did.

"Damn it!" Meisha grunted and snatched the car recklessly across four lanes of traffic. She came to a violent stop on the shoulder of the highway and turned in her seat. "Look here lil' nigga! You go in there stepping on toes and you gon' fuck up everything I got planned! It's my way or the highway! You can get your ass on a bus back to New York right now! I..."

"Ok, ok, dang," Bad Ass surrendered. "I'm just saying..."

"Don't say shit! Just fucking listen! With your...your..."

"Bad Ass?" Self slipped in between giggles. "A-yo I got him."

"Don't got him, get him. Before I do," Cameisha barked and put the car back in gear. She was still grumbling when she pulled back into I-20 traffic. Still mumbling when she exited on Candler Road and into Eastwyck.

"There go my Angel!" Self said proudly when he spotted Angel and Leera. Angel was a jet-black sixteen-year-old with thick hair down her back. The tiny white short set she wore almost seemed to glow in contrast to her dark skin. Light-skin Leera was as short and as thick as her friend was. She wore a matching short set in bright pink.

"Y'all little niggas be careful," Cameisha said sincerely. She tried to sound hard but failed.

"I got condoms," Self replied assuming that's what she meant. It was a classic half-truth. He did have a fresh three pack of lubed, ribbed, glow in the dark condoms but had no intention of using them.

"Yo, you don't think we should have a hammer?" Bad Ass asked when he got out of the car.

"For what? We ain't tryna take these niggas to war. We tryna ease in and take over," Meisha explained calmly. Naively actually. No way, they would be able to take over without bloodshed. This is the jungle and that's the law.

"Then I'ma put you and Self in charge out here. Y'all gon' run this," she said stroking his little ego. It worked too.

"That's what's up," he nodded with his chest out. Leera saw the smile on his face and assumed it was for her.

"Hey Bad Ass," she said making it sound like a lyric to a love ballad.

"Yeah, hey," he grumbled and accepted her hand as they made their way down the hill.

"My mama home," Angel pouted once their kiss ended. "She gon' be trippin.'"

"I'll holla at her. Yo, your brother home? I need to holla at him too," Self replied.

"What you need to talk to my brother about?" she wanted to know.

"Bout some business ma, be easy," he said calming her little nerves.

"I'll call him...later," she said indicating he was getting some ass first.

"After," he replied knowing he was getting some ass. As soon as they entered Angel's apartment her mother started bitching in the kitchen. Lil' Self went straight in to talk to her.

It wasn't much of a conversation. He merely retrieved four fat nicks from his pocket and extended his hand. The junky did a double take at the glass and passed gas.

"Excuse me," Ms. Johnson giggled. "Fo' me?"

"For you. You wouldn't mind if we all hang out over here would you? Smoke a blunt?" he asked sweetly. So sweetly, she couldn't say no.

"Not at all! Y'all have fun, I'm finna go smoke these with Mary!" Ms. Johnson proclaimed. She stood up and drained her water glass full of warm malt liquor then slid out the back door.

Self came back out and took Angel by the hand. They marched straight up the stairs to her bedroom.

"Hoe!" Leera called out playfully as if she wasn't about to do the same thing she was going to do.

"Come here," Bad Ass ordered the second they were alone. He pulled her on to his lap and stuck his tongue in her mouth. They kissed, grouped, and shed their clothes right there on the sofa. Leera generously put one foot on the floor and the other up on the back of the sofa. It was a formal introduction to her cervix. An invitation Bad Ass gladly accepted.

Bad Ass rolled a condom on and plunged inside of the girl. The youngin' had one speed, fast. The sound of skin slapping together filled the air and he slammed in and out of her like a jackhammer. At that rate, it didn't take long for him to grunt and fill his condom up. He grinded once or twice and jumped right up.

"I'm 'bout to hit the store," he announced standing up.

"Huh?" Leera asked accordingly. She knew she was a jump off, but that was a first. "Um...ok?"

Bad Ass waddled to the half-bath with his pants around his ankles. He pulled the condom off and tossed it in the toilet. Then he got a lesson on trying to clean off with toilet paper. In the end he stuck his dick under the faucet to remove the cum and stuck on tissue.

"Pick me up some Ju-Ju Beans, Starburst and orange..." Leera said trying to place her order as Bad Ass sped through the living room. He was out the door before she got it all out. With nothing else better to do, she snuck up the stairs to spy on her friend.

Leera practically grew up in that apartment so she knew which steps creaked loudly and avoided them. The raggedy old door to Angel's bedroom had a space between the jam, which allowed her to see straight in. She arrived to catch the end of an extended foreplay session. In other words, right on time for the action.

"So...we go together now?" Angel asked hopefully, between kisses. The teen might have been a little easy but she was no hoe. She was looking for love and sometimes you have to fuck to find it. Angel was a ride or die chick in the making. As soon as someone worthy came into her life she would ride or die.

"If you want," Self agreed. He was already smitten with the girl so why not lock her in. "Yeah you my girl."

Angel's panties got even wetter so she snatched them off and tossed them aside. She usually insisted upon condoms but allowed him inside of her raw. Leera felt a tinge of envy watching her friend make love.

She never made love, just got fucked. She longed for the face-to-face, eye contact, slow grind sex her friend was getting. She decided she would let Self make love to her too. He wouldn't be the first dude she fucked behind her friend.

The show ended when Self pushed deep inside and deposited half on a baby. Leera crept away as they kissed some more.

****

Bad Ass ventured out of the apartment and looked around. He spotted an obvious junkie and took note. The pep in her step meant she was going to cop so he fell in line behind her. She walked to the basketball court turned drug market. No one played ball anymore but you could get weed, pills, or crack. That was what he had been searching for.

"A-Yo, what's poppin' out here?" Bad Ass cheered, announcing his presence.

All the trapper's faces frowned at the intruder with the New York accent. They all looked around at each other to see who knew him. The frowns deepened when no one claimed him. He was officially bait.

"Who you here fo'? You tryna shop?" Lil Capo asked with his head cocked to the side.

"Yo I'm out here with a shawty. I just smashed so I came to see what the trap hitting on," he replied digging his hole deeper.

"What, you got yams?" Shawty asked. Shawty was called Shawty because he was short. He might have been 5'2" but he was a grown ass man. Physically anyway. The 35-year-old man went to prison at fifteen and came home twenty years later at seventeen years old mentally. He was out in the trap smoking, dancing, rapping, and trapping with kids young enough to be his kids. He went to prison for robbery and hadn't learned his lesson yet.

"Yams? Nah so. I got Jums!" Bad Ass flaunted and whipped out the work. That was the last thing he was going to remember. Shawty socked him so hard; he was sound asleep when he hit the ground.

"Damn this some fiyah!" Shawty celebrated when he pulled the dope out of his pocket. Devin shoved his hand in the other pocket and took what cash Bad Ass had.

That set off a chain reaction and everyone wanted to take something from the intruder. Capo snatched off his new sneakers while Tweek took the chain from his neck. Tamir pulled off his designer jeans while Stewart got the matching shirt.

"Where you going?" Capo asked Shawty as he eased away.

"I'm finna take this dope home. We can't let these smokers get a taste of this shit, not with that babbit Black feeding us!" he explained.

It sounded reasonable because it was half-true. They really couldn't afford for the junkies to get a taste of some good dope since they couldn't provide it on a regular. The other half was that Shawty was going to go smoke that shit.

"Oh yeah," Capo nodded, going for it. He sent his new shoes home and went back to trapping while Bad Ass slept.

****

"Where yo' friend at?" Angel asked her pouting friend as she limped downstairs. Self was right behind her with a smug look on his face since he gave her the limp.

"I'on know; said he was going to the sto'. That was awhile ago though," she answered. She gave Self a long, lustful glance that lingered on his crotch. Angel saw it and was about to check her until the front door suddenly swung open.

Ms. Johnson bust in looking wild and wide-eyed crazy.

"That's him!" she shouted and pointed right at Self. The poor kid was scared to death. He started to take off out the back door until he saw it was another junkie who came in behind her and not the police or jackers. "That's that nigga that gave me that good ass dope!"

"You gave my mama some dope?" Angel whined. She knew her mother was a junkie but tried her best to save her. Truth be told, there was no saving her. She, like a lot of addicts wouldn't be free until her casket closed.

"Chile leave him 'lone. You can't keep no man by nagging him!" her mama chided. At least that part was true. Y'all listen to Mama and stop nagging. "Come on in the kitchen."

Self followed Ms. Johnson into the kitchen with Mary right behind him to make sure he couldn't get away. He shrugged helplessly at Angel as he left.

"Let me get 'fo!" Mary yelled extending a fresh twenty in her beat up old hand that looked like a monkey paw.

That sale set off a chain reaction. Word of the good dope spread like a wild fire. Mama Johnson ran back and forth making a smokable commission off each sale. Once the word hit the trap, someone called Black.

"What happened to you?" Leera shouted when a half-naked Bad Ass came through the door.

"Them niggas robbed me," he said to Self as if he was the one who asked. Self just shook his head and grabbed his phone.

"A-yo Meish, come through. We may have a problem."

Chapter 10

Self was notoriously bad at keeping his phone charged. The device was useless more often than useful. It cut off halfway through him explaining what happened. She wasn't sure what was going on, so she grabbed a tech-nine along with a change of clothes for Bad Ass.

Trigga was on the west side handling his business and Jackie was caught up as well. Aqua was pregnant so she went alone. Then again, with thirty-rounds in the clip you're not really alone.

Meisha's busy mind ran through all kinds of possible scenarios as she raced towards Decatur. It dawned on her then how much she cared about the little misfits. They were the little brothers she never had. And if anything happened to them, she was going to murder whoever did it. Her foot sank further on the gas as she sped to Eastwyck.

"Something going on fo' sho!" Black explained to his right hand man Sparks sitting beside him. He got word that some good dope was coming out of his Mama's house and he knew good and damn well he didn't have any good dope. It wasn't unusual for him to drop a bomb off for his mother to hustle and smoke on, but it was the same babbit he pushed off on the trap boys.

When he got the word, he went to investigate. He parked his donk across the street and watched. Watched his mother scurry to and fro higher than the 30-inch rims on the Chevy. The candy colored car didn't even register to Cameisha when she pulled up. She slammed the Benz in park and hopped out.

"Damn that bitch got a fat ass!" Sparks shouted and clapped. A fat ass does deserve a round of applause after all.

"Can't be no smoker," Black agreed. She was also a little too old to be friends with his sister so he got out to investigate.

"Hey," Angel sang warmly as she opened the door. Self had spoken so highly and so much of his big sister that she loved her too.

"Sup yo," Meisha shot back scanning the room for danger as she stepped inside. She gripped the Tech tightly in the large designer purse containing Bad Ass' clothes. Anything or anyone out of place would have caught a three shot burst from the machine pistol. Her eyes settled on Bad Ass nearly naked on the sofa. "What's going on?"

"That's what I wanna know," Black said as he entered behind her. Meisha spun around and almost fired through the bag until she saw both men's empty hands.

"He got jumped," Self explained while Bad Ass pouted.

"By who? Why? Where they at? Why?" she growled down at him.

"Oh you the one came through the trap?" Black laughed since news of that had reached him as well.

"The trap? You was in the trap? What part of go slow, be easy, don't you understand?" Cameisha scolded with Sparks' eyes glued to her ass.

"Uh...who are you? Why y'all in my mama's house?" Black interjected.

"This my boyfriend, his brother, and their sister!" Angel said protectively rushing to Self's side.

"Ok, so, who 'posed to be selling dope out of here?" he inquired twisting his lips and cocking his head.

"No one. We just..."

"I need five mo'!" Mama rushed in cutting Self off before he could finish his lie. All eyes shot to him for explanation. He shrugged and served her since the cat was out of the bag.

"Hol' up Mama, let me see that," Black frowned at the dope. It wasn't one of those frowns people make when they're upset. It was the kind dudes make when they see a fat ass. The kind Sparks still wore because he was still staring at Cameisha's ass. "Wow! Where you get this shit from lil' man?" Black asked turning back to Self.

"Me!" Cameisha answered for him. "I...my people got a good connect on some good dope. Holla at me if you tryna shop."

"Um, excuse me. You bring me some clothes?" Bad Ass finally spoke up.

"Here," she answered pulling a pair of jeans and shirt from out of the purse. "I ain't know you needed shoes. Self let him wear your sneakers." Lil' Self didn't flinch at the odd command. He kicked his sneakers off and sat them in front of Bad Ass.

"We need to talk a lil' business," Black offered.

"First things first. My brother gotta go straighten his face. We can't go out like that yo," Meisha explained.

"I respect that," Black nodded. "We can go 'round to the trap and let him handle his business. I'll make sure no one jumps in."

"So will I," she said to Sparks' amusement. He chuckled at the cute girl thinking she could prevent the young wolves from eating the boy if they chose to do so. That's because he didn't have x-ray vision and couldn't see the Tech-9 in the bag.

Bad Ass had absolutely no bitch in him. Not a trace. When Black hit the door, he was right behind him. Sparks allowed Cameisha to go ahead of him so he could stare at her ass some more. Self and the girls were in the rear.

"Here come that lil' nigga," Devin laughed until his mind registered Black and the rest.

His mind was too slow to process the information so he shrugged and waited for someone to explain it to him. Black opened his mouth to speak, but Cameisha beat him to it.

"A-yo, which one of y'all jumped my brother?" she demanded with her hand in the bag. No one present had any idea how close to a massacre they were at that second. The wrong word and Cameisha would have aired it out.

"Look shawty, that nigga came through the trap and tried to set up shop. He gotta respect the game," Capo explained.

"Oh we respect the game. Now he wants a one with everybody who touched him!" she shot back.

"Say no more," Tweek said still wearing Bad Ass's chain. As soon as he stepped up Bad Ass bombed on him.

The punch staggered the teen, but he came right back. He traded punches evenly until they both were knotted up pretty good. It was a close fight so Black stepped in and broke it up.

"Give him his shit back," Black insisted. Tweek huffed and puffed, but complied. He handed both the chain along with his respect to Bad Ass.

"You too," he said and socked Stewart in his jaw. Stewart was a little too much for him and got him down. Once the fight was reduced to a wrestling match, Black broke it up too.

Next came Tamir, Devin, and Capo. Bad Ass fought all of them win, lose, or draw. Shawty arrived on the scene as Black pried Capo and Bad Ass apart. As soon as Bad Ass saw him, he went for him too.

"A-yo, hold up!" Cameisha shouted when she got a closer look at Shawty. She took him for a teen due to his height, but up close, she saw the frown lines in his face and a trace of grey in his temples. "Nigga how old are you?"

"He old enough to be my daddy," Tamir ratted. He was no snitch but he couldn't stand the grown man who hung out with them.

"Bitch who you 'posed to be," Shawty quizzed balling his fist up. He was high as a kite from smoking the good dope and feeling no pain. Not yet anyway.

"Your old ass out here robbing kids? Self hold my purse," she insisted. Self started to complain about holding a purse until he saw the Tech inside.

"I ain't finna fight no bitch," Shawty griped and got punched right in his mouth. He opened his mouth to speak and got popped again. "Bitch!" Shawty yelled and attacked. Dude had a mean sucker punch game but couldn't fight a lick. He swung wildly and paid dearly for every punch.

Cameisha went into counterpunch mode and punished him every time he swung. She would either duck, dip, or dodge a looping punch then deliver combinations consisting of jabs, hooks, and uppercuts.

"Damn that bitch got a fat ass!" Sparks insisted once more.

"Damn that bitch can fight," Black responded as she thoroughly whooped Shawty's ass. That one he wouldn't break up because he didn't have much respect for Shawty either.

Actually, he didn't have to break it up because Cameisha intended to beat him to sleep. A Mike Tyson-esque uppercut lifted him up and dropped him right on his ass. If he hadn't had so much coke in his system he would have been sound asleep. Instead, he lay flat on his back, eyes wide open, daydreaming.

"Now, let's go talk business," Meisha said switching back to dope girl mode.

****

"So check it, how much y'all paying for ounces now?" Cameisha asked once they were seated in his mama's kitchen.

"Shit...like five hundred," Black lied. She knew it was some bullshit and the shocked expression on Sparks' face confirmed it. She knew right then he would never, ever do straight business. It just wasn't in him.

"Ok, a couple things. First, no, you're not paying five hundred an ounce. Second, you should be because your product is wack. Garbage, trash. You see for yourself how that glass got 'em," Cameisha laid out. "Now if I let you get them for the same $750, $700 if you cop ten or better, you'll make the same dough but get more customers because you got the best dope around."

"Damn, this bitch knows her shit!" Sparks cheered. He actually meant it as a compliment, but only dumb bitches take being called a bitch as a compliment. Go try it on your mother or grandmother if you don't believe me. March on into the kitchen and say 'bitch you did your thing with these biscuits'.

"Oh! There's a third thing," she said turning toward Sparks. "If you ever call me a bitch again we gon' fight."

"Shit, my bad shawty," he laughed holding his hands up as if it were a stick up. He might have been laughing, but knew she was serious after the way she laid hands on Shawty.

"So how much you let a whole bird go for then?" Black asked to test how deep the river ran.

"For you...twenty-five," she replied which equaled $700 an ounce.

"Shit, Playboy charging twenty-seven!" Sparks blurted out exposing their whole operation. First, if they were paying that much per key, they were several middlemen away from the connect. Next, there hadn't been a black connect in Atlanta since Cameron Forrest died, or whatever.

"A'ight, so let me get like five of them tomorrow," Black said giving him time to knock off the rest of his garbage. The $3750 was about what he was paying currently for four ounces of trash. He wasn't the sharpest knife in the drawer, but knew this was a come up.

"Five keys no problem, I'll be..."

"No! Five ounces," he cut in and cut her off. It wasn't really necessary, since she was just chumping him off. She knew good and well he couldn't afford it, but wanted him to know she had it.

"Oh, one more thing. My brothers get to work the trap too. They gotta eat."

"No problem. Shawty earned his respect. Ain't nare nigga gon' fuck wit' them," Black vowed.

"That's what's up," Meisha said as she stood. Sparks' eyes locked onto her ass as she left the room.

The boys got last kisses and feels and followed her out. Poor Angel looked like she wanted to cry when Self left. Back in the kitchen, Black was deep in thought.

"You really gon' shop with this broad?" Sparks asked, carefully avoiding the B-word.

"For a sec. I'ma see what this bitch working with. If she getting bricks like that I may have to fuck her, or rob her ass," he laughed. Sparks found it real fucking funny but his sister didn't.

In fact, she was disgusted by it. She loved her boyfriend and admired his sister. She wouldn't let her trifling brother hurt either one.

Chapter 11

"What happened to you?" Trigga asked seeing Cameisha come in with blood on her sweat pants.

"It ain't mine. I had to put hands on some nigga," she laughed.

"Him?" Trigga frowned as a lumped up Bad Ass walked in behind her. "You ever eat one of these?"

"Um, no and hell no!" she grimaced seeing him munching on a Fat-Fat burger. Aqua sat beside him on the sofa with her mouthful of the greasy, meaty, cheesy burger. Still she managed a smile and a wave.

"I'm surprised to see she shared with you," Meisha continued. She was still frowning from the memory of the taste in her mouth.

"The last one too! I'ma take her to get more," he said proudly and took another bite squirting juice onto the coffee table.

"You are?" she asked in amusement. Aqua just nodded up and down while she chewed. Cameisha knew he got duped, but kept quiet, for the moment.

"Yup, oh! And I need another one of them thangs," he said lifting his chin in nobility.

"Already? Dope boy fo' real!" she laughed and headed to the bedroom. She tossed him a look that told him he should come too. He could tell it was business, not sexual, and followed her in.

"Well, I got a plug in the trap in Eastwyck. Self's girlfriend's brother. He feeding the trap and I'm supplying him," she explained.

"Can you trust him?" he asked protectively.

"Nah, he gon' fuck up. Just a matter of time. I can't wait, and then I can take over! What you got going on?"

"Got Oak Tree on lock. Once word spread, the rest them 'partments gon' come on in," he answered correctly. Once the other dealer felt the pinch in their pockets, they would have no choice but to switch suppliers. Of course, the old suppliers would have a problem with that, but that's what guns are for.

"Any word on a connect? Once we get all this shit poppin' we gon' need a steady supply. A couple bricks a day easy," he went on.

Cameisha twisted her lips as she racked her brain for an answer. The music from "Jeopardy" played in her mind, but nothing came.

"I'll come up with something," she vowed. The coke she had on hand was worth over a half a million, but she still wanted more. "So, when you going to Mississippi?"

"Mississippi? Why would I be going to Mississippi?" he wondered.

"You taking Aqua to get more burgers right?"

"Hell yeah! Them shits are delicious!" he cheered pumping a fist.

"Well they can only be found in Longs, Mississippi. Drive safe," she said and finally cracked up. "You gotta keep your word yo. You told her you was gonna take her so you gotta take her!"

"Come with me," Trigga pleaded. His word was his bond so there was no question that he would keep it.

"To Mississippi?" she asked almost frightened. "Nah, I ain't never going back there again."

Trigga heard all that she didn't say and let it go. Even when she mentally drifted away, he didn't press. Instead, he took her into his arms. He laid her down beside him and soon they both fell sound asleep.

****

When the good dope hit Eastwyck the next day, the effect was drastic, instant, and irreversible. Once the junkies got a blast of that good, they would no longer settle for mediocre. Black proved Cameisha right and was two hundred dollars short on his purchase. He handed her a roll of cash as if she wouldn't count it. She did.

"Either you can't count or think I can't" she growled so ferociously he could smell the malice on her breath.

"Oh, my bad," he chuckled like it was an accident but handed over the exact amount of the short.

"No problem," she lied. The smile might have been fake but she really was quite pleased that he tried her. She passed off the dope and gave him something to look at when she walked out.

"Be careful," Cameisha told Self before she left. She gave him a smooch on the forehead to tease Angel and punched Bad Ass.

"Bye," Angel sang sisterly, unfazed by the kiss. Why should she be when she was about to take him upstairs and fuck him silly?

She didn't bother telling Bad Ass to be careful since she knew good and damn well he wouldn't be. He was that one friend you couldn't take anywhere. The second Cameisha pulled off, he headed for the trap.

"What's up shawty," Capo nodded when Bad Ass arrived on the scene. He wasn't officially the leader, but he was the coolest so his acceptance meant something.

"What up yo," he greeted back. When the two exchanged a pound and man hug, the rest lined up to do the same. All except Shawty that is. He held a grudge about getting his ass handed to him by a girl. Plus he was too busy looking for that girl to be shaking hands.

Bad Ass had no problem sharing sales since he had more dope than everyone else. He slipped into the rotation and took turns serving the junkies. Whenever they ran out the trap would be his until whenever Black could re-up from Cameisha. He had an inside source that it wouldn't be that night. He also had a quarter key of good, hard dope.

Meanwhile back at the apartment Self was busy getting pussy whipped. It was a win/win since Mama was handling sales to her crack head friends, and he was getting pussy whipped. They both heard Mama run in and call for Self. They hoped she wouldn't come upstairs, but no luck.

"Self, Self, I need 12 for the fiddy son-in-law," she requested through the crack in the door as if the couple wasn't copulating.

"Mama!" Angel screamed from embarrassment and her fucking up an impending orgasm. She was so close and it slipped away.

"Give me a few minutes!" Self shouted and stayed focused. His stroke grew choppy indicating that the end was near.

"Throw it back girl! You just lying there. Throw it back!" Mama coached from the hallway.

"Mama!" Angel yelled again just as Self got off.

"That was a good one!" she announced and stepped down the creaky steps.

"Yo, your moms is wild!" Self laughed after he pulled out and got up. She silently watched him get dressed and go serve her mother. He retrieved some of the dope he stashed in her closet and hit the steps.

"I need 12 for the fiddy," she repeated so there would be no misunderstanding. She was making two rocks off the top plus whatever the customer paid her for making the run. Ms. Johnson was in the junkie-loop and brought in as many sales as the trap boys could make.

With her running sales he was free to cuddle up with his boo and let the money come to him. It was time to bring his clothes and move in.

****

"A Fat-Fat burger?" Troy frowned when Trigga delivered news of his day trip along with dope for the day. Aqua snapped her head at the mention of her Fat-Fat.

"I promised," he replied which summed it up. Troy knew him his whole life and he hadn't broken one yet. "Shit, I'll be back by this evening."

"Oh don't worry, I got this!" he replied rubbing his hands together eagerly. He had made a playdate with the next hoe in line at Oak Tree. He was on a mission and Ta-Ta was her name. She pushed up on him the night before when he made his last collections.

Troy distributed the work to the workers in his complex then sped over to Oak Tree. As soon as he pulled in, he saw the black beauty waiting with a hand on her wide hip. She slid into the passenger seat while he passed out the G-packs.

"Lick his balls girl, he like that!" Nita-Boo coached from the sidelines.

"You know I'm is!" she shot back. She was all douched, dressed, and ready to go.

Troy took a hard look at her thick black thighs when he got back in his car. He felt his dick jump and put the car in gear. He stopped at the same corner store and sent her inside for a bottle of Real Nigga 9000. It was about to go down!

They pulled up to the same hotel and got a similar room with similar stains on the comforter. Troy dropped his jeans and pulled his shirt over his head.

"You brang me that? Ta-Ta asked as she began to peel off her skimpy clothing. Troy heard her speaking but couldn't process the words because of her banging body.

Ta-Ta might have been the next hoe on the hoe-tum pole but she and Nita-Boo were polar opposites. Instead of high yellow, tall, and long hair she was jet black, short with short hair gelled down on her scalp. She pulled off her wife beater and shorts and did a spin so he could see that her bra and panties didn't match. She unhooked the white bra to show off the big black titties with her large lumpy areolas and long suckable nipples. She pulled off the pink panties to display a bush of thick pubic hair.

"Well?" she asked again as he stared at her crotch with the crop on top.

"Well what?" he asked coming out of the trance.

"You said you was gon' brang me some powder," she said in her little girl voice. The one little girls use to get anything out of their daddies. Ta-Ta never met her daddy so she used it on sugar daddies instead.

"Oh! Yeah, yeah here you go," he replied and went into his pants pocket. He retrieved one of the two one-gram packages he had brought for her. The other one he would give her once he dropped her back off.

"Thank ya," she said taking the dope from his hand. Her own hand trembled in anticipation of the get high.

Troy leaned back and lit a blunt as Ta-Ta dumped the coke on the table. She made two thick lines and quickly inhaled. She took a swig from the 60-ounce bottle like a real nigga and made two more lines.

"Whew! This that shit!" she frowned and pointed at the drugs.

She had become used to the local coke that was cut to smithereens. The dealers cut the coke with baby laxative so people would have to shit and swear it was because the dope was good. Even though she was high, she still snorted two more lines. That was where she fucked up.

"You better not come quick!" she warned climbing on the bed. She grabbed his dick and watched it swell in her hand then took it in her mouth. Ta-Ta slowly inched him down her throat like a snake does its meals.

Troy enjoyed watching the blowjob for awhile before pulling her up. She had the kind of ass you have to hit from behind so that's how he positioned her. Once he rolled a condom safely in place, he fell inside her well-used vagina. It squished and farted as he stroked.

"I'm finna cum," Ta-Ta whined like she didn't want to. She coated his dick with creamy juice and began to shake. She grunted as she came and then went stiff.

"Un uh, don't run," Troy laughed when she collapsed on the bed. He turned her over to put her in the buck, but saw foam coming out of her mouth and nostrils. He leaped clear off the bed from shock. "What the world!"

"Ta-Ta, Ta-Ta!" he called down at her. He got louder and louder and finally touched her. Nothing, so he took her pulse. Nothing, so he got dressed and got the fuck up out of there.

"Where my girl at?" Nita-Boo asked when Troy returned alone.

"She um...was sleep at the hotel," he replied leaving out the eternal part.

"Mmph, you must have put it on her! Shoot...she was 'posed to share some of that powder!" she pouted.

"I ain't fuck her! Still got the powder see!" he exclaimed and produced the other package. Nita-Boo snatched it and ran around the car and hopped in. she went straight for his zipper so he leaned back and let her blow him on the spot.

Chapter 12

"Another one? How can this be?" Anna asked the dead girl on the table. She knew the nineteen-year-old girl didn't just drop dead from a heart attack. Besides an STD and beat up vagina, Ta-Ta was healthy.

The test on the cocaine found with her and in her at the motel tested positively back to the Salazar family product. The black girl was the second one that week. An older crack addict was laying in a drawer with the same drug in her abused system.

It was time to speak to Juan again. She would not be able to keep it under wraps for much longer. Anna longed to reveal that Cameisha was his sister, but she would not cross Mama Salazar. The woman scared her so much she shook her head no at the very thought of disobeying her.

"Anna?" Juan asked with a curious frown just as he reached his destination. It was unusual for her to call him and he didn't have time to socialize. "I am very busy now. I will..."

"It is very important! I must speak with you now!" she shot back firmly. "Where are you? We cannot speak on the phone."

"I just reached the green house. Meet me at Mama's tonight."

"I'll come to you now. I mu..."

"No!" Juan shouted. She had been to that house before but he didn't want her to see what he had going on now. "At mi madre, tonight!"

"Que pasa? Ju ok?" David asked with his best English.

"Where is the girl?" Juan asked in response. He scanned the living room before turning to face his help.

"In de room," he answered pointing at a small monitor on the table. Juan frowned again then went and looked at the screen.

"Why is she naked?" he asked seeing Samantha in her makeshift lab. One of the master bedrooms had been fitted with all of the equipment she ordered to comply with her orders. A small daybed was installed for her to sleep.

"Like de New Yack City," David nodded and smiled happily. If he had a tail, it would be wagging just then. He almost got a smack instead of a pat on the head.

"Open the door!" he demanded wiping the smile away.

David rushed to comply and unlocked the deadbolt installed to convert the bedroom into a prison.

"This would have been sufficient!" he chided pointing at the heavy-duty lock.

"It's about time! I...uh oh," Samantha began then stopped. Juan had already hit her twice. She was in no hurry to make it three.

"I came to...um? Damn!" he said but got stuck by her nudity. Her big creamy white breasts had cute pink nipples that stood erect from the chill. A shock of blonde pubic hair hid her plump vagina. "David bring her some clothes," he ordered. David took one final mental snapshot of her bare body and took off.

"I am truly sorry about this but it is Cameisha's fault! She has betrayed us all," Juan explained. He knew his captive would see things his way since he was her savior.

"She is a very selfish person," Samantha pouted. "I just do what I'm told to do."

"I see," he replied seeing four neat bricks of cocaine on the lab table. He sent one, now there was four. The white lab rat in the cage caught his attention so he went over to investigate. The little fellow was in his wheel running 65 miles an hour. "Is it sweating?"

"Probably, he's been at it for two hours!" she laughed. David came in with a t-shirt and handed it to Juan.

"This is the only thing I could find," he explained.

"Go to the mall and buy her clothes! What size?" he asked pulling out cash to make the purchase.

"Well..." Samantha began and started to go in, but changed her mind. "A seven is fine. Eight in shoes please."

Juan handed her the shirt and missed her pretty titties as soon as they disappeared behind the fabric. Still he got stuck on the imprint caused by her nipples. Samantha saw him and saw her way out of her predicament.

"I'm very sorry about your girlfriend," she pouted and moved in for a hug. She pulled him tightly against her and rocked and grinded ever so slightly.

Juan's body betrayed him when it felt the feel of a woman. He was powerless to stop the erection growing in between them.

"I'm sorry," he muttered in embarrassment and tried to pull away. Either Samantha was too strong or he was too weak because she held him in place. "What are you doing?"

"I...don't know," she whispered and tilted her head upwards in case he wanted to kiss her. Turned out that was exactly what he wanted and he took the bait.

"Look it," David giggled to himself as he watched the show. It only got better when she sank to her knees. She scrambled to free his erection only to take it deep into her mouth.

Juan didn't stand a chance against white girl head. Most head is good but white girl head is great! Between the stress of losing his woman and impending war, Juan was a bundle of nerves. He exploded so hard against her tonsils that she gagged loudly. Gagged, but hung in there.

"Mmm," Samantha moaned as she drank him down. His knees buckled almost causing him to fall. She rose and led him to the bed. He was all hers now and she knew it. He knew it too and didn't try to fight it. The t-shirt came back off.

"Wait!" she shouted to himself and snatched the small camera off the wall. That ended the show for David so he slunk out of the house.

One good deed deserves another so Juan leaned towards the pretty pink vagina to pay it forward. He flicked his tongue at her clit making her vagina blossom like a flower. Her whole body shook when he licked her slippery lips. Samantha was pretty uptight about being kidnapped and all so she didn't last too long either. She repaid him by coming in his mouth as well.

A condom wasn't even in the equation when he scrambled to put himself inside of her. Samantha was already tight from infrequent sex, so when she squeezed her muscles even more the effect was virginal.

"Are you ok?" Juan asked as he eased inside of her.

"Yes, it hurts. I only did it once you know," she lied making him come instantly. He gasped for air from the sudden violent orgasm.

"Mm baby," Samantha purred and stroked his back. "Now what?"

"Now..." Juan twisted his lips in contemplation. "For now, you stay here. Keep manufacturing the cocaine. Once this is over, once Cameisha is dead, you will be my queen."

****

"Un uh, I can't," Dasia scowled when she caught Uncle Mark jacking off while smelling her panties. She and Lisa had only been at Big Mama's house for a couple of days when she reached her limit. Between the dope fiend and small army of children, it was only a matter of time until her cache of drugs or stash of cash was discovered.

Lisa wasn't quite sure how much of either Dasia had but she was determined to run through it as quickly as humanly possible. First, they rented a two thousand dollar a month condo. Dasia figured they could live there for years off what she had taken. Boy was she wrong.

"I like this one," Lisa said pointing at a blue leather sofa and love seat.

"Get it," Dasia nodded nonchalantly at the five thousand dollar price tag. She dropped another five thousand to furnish the one bedroom. A few more thousand filled the dining room and kitchen. By the time they threw in electronics, they spent over fifteen thousand, but Lisa wasn't done yet.

"You hear that?" Lisa asked as she drove along the boulevard.

"Hear what?" Dasia asked wondering how she could hear anything over the loud music. Even once she twisted the volume down, she couldn't hear anything. "What?"

"Girl you don't hear that?" she asked again and pulled into the next parking lot. It just so happened to be the local Lexus dealer.

"How can I help you ladies?" a handsome young black man in a handsome blue suit asked. He was a salesman there but the brilliant white smile was free.

"It was grinding," Lisa swore with a faux damsel in distress tone that Dasia found a little odd. Had she not smoked a blunt for breakfast and again with lunch she would have seen through the charade.

"It may be time to step up. I'm William," he said offering his hand along with his name.

"Um, Dasia. This is Lisa," Dasia introduced. After the test drive, even Dasia had to agree it was time to step up.

"But it's forty thousand," Lisa pouted to Dasia.

"We'll take it!" she announced and to both their surprise retrieved her tote bag full of cash. Had Lisa known it was there Dasia would have woken up alone at Big Mama's house.

"We can't take that much cash," William explained. He sent her across the street to open an account.

"Don't put it all in there," Lisa whined. Even she heard the greed in her voice and made an adjustment. "I'm saying; keep like ten in cash so we don't gotta keep running back and forth."

"Ok," Dasia agreed. Fortunately, Lisa's credit was too bad to be added to the account. She had to settle for an ATM card, which would limit her plan to drain the account to one thousand dollars a day.

After getting a 43 thousand dollar cashier's check, they left over eighty grand in the bank. Lisa and William traded a wink once the car was in her name. William was an old friend and made a nice commission on the sale. He would sell her old car and split the proceeds with her.

Dasia got something out of the deal too. Lisa sucked a nut right out of her when they got home. Of course, Dasia the doormat returned the favor and put them both down for a nap. They awoke hours later and smoked a blunt.

"I want some powder," Lisa whined. She knew Dasia had taken some coke along with several pounds of weed but she hadn't set it out yet. In her mind, it was the final line to be crossed. If Cameisha kicked the door in right then at least she could give it back. She knew Cameisha was coming one day, but still she agreed.

"Ok," Dasia gave in. It didn't take much pressing since she was thirsty for some coke herself. She pulled a couple of ounces out by eye to part with. "We still need to sell them."

"We will," Lisa agreed and snorted a long, thick line up each nostril. "But tonight, we party!"

****

"I'ma stunt on these hoes!" Lisa vowed as she squeezed into a short designer dress. She had left there in disgrace so that night was her redemption song. Lisa snorted two big hits and climbed up into her high heel shoes.

"You sure your friend will buy it?" Dasia asked slightly worried at how much coke they'd used that day. She didn't need to be since Lisa had cuffed a good deal of it. Still, they had an ounce to take to the club.

"Cash Money is always in the club," she assured her. "You looking good girl!"

Dasia looked in the mirror and saw she was right. She was killing the designer tube dress that showed off her every curve.

"We need all that cash?" Dasia shrieked seeing her stuff thousands in her purse.

"Nah, it's just for show, and we finna show out!" she lied. After all, it ain't tricking when it's someone else's money. A few more hits of coke later and they were on their way.

As soon as they neared the club, Lisa rolled down the windows and turned up the radio. She pulled slowing through the parking lot and stopped at the valet parking. All eyes were on the two pretty girls who emerged from the pretty car with the dealer sticker still attached.

"Is that Li-Li?" an old classmate asked squinting so she could see better.

"You mean bum ass Li-Li who got on the dope and ran off with Cash Money's cash money?" her friend replied.

Lisa turned in their direction and ended the speculation.

"Rita? Tina?" Lisa gushed like they were closer than they really were. They once ran in the same circle but were never really friends. "Y'all get out that long ass line and come with us!"

The girls gladly got out of the line and followed Lisa to the VIP entrance. She paid fifty bucks a head for them to bypass the line. A hundred dollar tip granted them access to the VIP area along with the other ghetto celebrities. Five hundred more got five bottles of champagne delivered to the table.

"So what you doing now girl?" Tina wanted to know. This was the same chick who left looking a mess a year earlier and now she had run through a grand in ten minutes. Again, it ain't tricking when it's someone else's money. No one knew that better than she did.

"Girl I finally got a record deal!" she said causing Dasia's head to snap in her direction. It wasn't the lie so much that caught her attention. It was how easily it flowed. It sounded just like any of their everyday conversation. She listened as Lisa detailed in great detail a bunch of shit that wasn't true.

"Oh, there go Cash Money," Rita warned causing an uncomfortable hush to fall over the table. Dasia scanned everyone's face trying to figure out what she missed.

She wasn't from there and didn't know the history. How many hoes move to a new town and get a clean slate? Lisa had been popular in the dope boy circles for her wicked head game. Not only could she suck a dick, but eat pussy just as proficiently. Dope boys would call her over to take care of them and their girlfriends. Somewhere along the way, she picked up a bad dope habit. She started by snorting, then smoking, and finally shooting heroin.

One night after sucking Cash Money to sleep, she ran off with ten thousand dollars' worth of dope plus a few grand from his pocket.

"Just the man I was looking for," she announced and stood. She grabbed her purse and marched off.

Dasia watched her walk away but saw Rita scooping coke out of the package they set out. She just shook her head as if she didn't even see it.

"Sup Cash Money. Looking for me?" she asked with hand on hip.

"Is that...I know it ain't...Bitch you better have my damn money!" Cash Money growled. The man was a known killer and would have killed her on the spot. Choked her ass out right there in the VIP and no one would have said shit.

"Of course I got your money! That's why I been looking for you," she giggled girlishly.

"Well bitch, let's have it," he demanded.

"It's in the car. I need to holla at you 'bout some business anyway."

"First get me my money! Matter fact I'm coming with you," he said standing. Two of his goons stood too but he waved them back down. Instead of watching his back, they watched her backside as they left.

"I see you bounced back," Cash Money said watching her toss her ass from side to side in front of him. The dope had her on the verge of extinction before she ran off. She actually sold the dope she stole and got clean once she got to Atlanta.

"Can't keep a good bitch down," she replied and slung her ass a little harder since she knew he was watching. She bent over into the car and let him palm her ass while she retrieved the cash.

"This ain't but five grand," he said dead on accurate without even counting it. His name was Cash Money after all.

"Yeah, daddy, I don't be riding around with no ten bands. I wasn't sure if I was gon' see you either. I'll brang you the change in the morning," she offered hopefully.

"Tomorrow?" he asked cocking his head dubiously. He glanced at the price on the sticker and gave in. "Tomorrow."

"That's a bet, but 'bout that business. My people got a key they tryna get off. Don't want but fifteen."

"Girl you know I don't fuck with no coke. I push that boy."

"Oh boy," she replied feeling her stomach churn at the mention of heroin.

"Matter fact, come to my truck. Let me break you off a lil' something."

"I um, I stop...I don't fuck around no mo'," she mumbled to herself but still followed him to his custom SUV. She climbed in the backseat with him and closed the door.

"First things first," he said and leaned back to pull his dick out. She knew not sucking it wasn't an option so she grabbed it and leaned in.

"Dang!" she giggled feeling it stiffen in her hand from anticipation alone. It had been over a year since she gave a guy head but they say it's just like riding a bike.

"Yeah you still got it," he moaned when she twirled her wet tongue around his dick head while stroking the shaft. Knowing Dasia would be upset if she was gone too long, she got busy. She threw her head and hand into overdrive in a rush to get him off. It wasn't long until his dick spasms filled her mouth with hot, salty cum. She swallowed in loud gulps while milking him dry with her hand.

"Here you go lil' mama," Cash Money said seductively as he passed her a few balloons of dope. Lisa was on autopilot as she accepted them and put it in her purse. "I'll see you tomorrow. Brang the coke too."

"Tomorrow," she repeated and hopped from the truck. She made a beeline to the club and slipped back inside. She hoped she wouldn't be noticed, but Dasia was keeping watch on the door. The moment she stepped back in, they met eyes. Only for a second though because Dasia rolled hers and turned away.

Rita and Tina were so busy trying to snort and steal as much cocaine as they could they didn't know she was gone. Dasia was already hot, but when Lisa leaned in for a kiss, she snapped.

"Ew! I can smell cum on your breath!" she fumed. Dasia had sucked enough dicks to know the smell and taste. "Shit I may as well just go suck his dick and cut out the middle man!"

"Girl shush!" Lisa scolded. Rita and Tina kept right on snorting like Kermit sips tea. "You think I sucked that nigga's dick for me! You think I did it for him? Nah, girl, I sucked that dick for you!"

"Me?" Dasia exclaimed. "Please explain to me how you gave a nigga some head, for me!"

"Everything in this city goes through him. We wouldn't be able to sell a damn thing without his permission. He wanted to fuck me but this is your pussy," she said pulling her hand under her dress. Dasia couldn't help but to fondle it and felt it moisten her fingers. "Yours girl, what you gonna do with it?"

"Let's go home," she purred in a whisper. Lisa stood for a reply and led her out of the club. Her friends high-fived at the free dope.

Chapter 13

"Sss, don't cum in me," Angel hissed when Self's body told her was close. His moans increased and breath grew ragged, he was almost there. The plea sounded sincere, urgent almost, but it was a lie. That girl knew good and well she wanted him to cum in her. She had every intention of becoming his baby mama. It was moot at that point since she was already pregnant. Just hadn't missed that period that wasn't coming.

"Ok," he agreed and attempted to pull out. Once again, Angel grabbed him tightly and prevented his escape. Truth be told, he wanted her to be his baby mama too and had no problem exploding inside her. He pushed in all the way grinding as he came. She squeezed and rocked to make sure she got all of it. Even reached an orgasm of her own for good measure. Neither moved until Self deflated inside of her and was squeezed out.

"Yo, go grab us a soda. I'll roll another blunt," he said rolling off her onto his back.

"Yo go grab us a soda, yo, yo, yo," she mocked playfully as she got up to comply. She stepped into a pair of panties then pulled his t-shirt over her head.

"Bad Ass still here?" Self asked with a frown. He did not want his friend seeing his girl half-naked. That's the respect part of love. A man who lets his woman prance around naked in public can't have much respect for her. Himself either for that matter.

"Un uh, I heard them leave," she replied stifling a smile. She knew it was honor and not jealousy that made him ask.

Bad Ass and Leera had been downstairs earlier. He fucked her so quickly she couldn't even get undressed. Just one pants leg out and it was on. He bust a quick nut and hit the trap.

Angel paused at the top of the stairs when she heard voices below. She recognized her brother and Sparks so she crept forward to ear hustle. After stepping over the creaky step, she silently made her way downstairs. Black had been using the kitchen table to cut dope and plan a lick.

"So how we 'posed to get her and she not know it's us?" Sparks wondered. He was down with the plan but secretly feared the girl.

"Ok, we got the bitch up to a quarter now so I'ma tell her I need a whole thing. When she brang it, Shawty come in the back wearing a mask and lay all of us down."

"He gon' rob us too?" Sparks shouted. "I ain't tryna get robbed no more. Them niggas on Glenwood got me for..."

"Nigga! We gon' get our shit back. We gotta go along so she don't know we was down with the lick. Shit, we wait a month or so and get her ass again!" Black explained.

He was smiling but his sister wasn't. She had to cover her own mouth to stop herself from speaking out. Luckily, she was able to contain herself to hear the rest of the plan.

"I feel you. So, what we gon' do with the key? That shit gon' look suspect if all of a sudden we got work," Sparks advised.

"Man it's plenty niggas tryna buy kilos. The market fucked up right now. We can sell it for the high-high!" Black cheered.

He was right too because the Salazars controlled the cocaine flow and had yet to crank back up. Juan was too busy having Samantha flip the coke they had. Once that was done, they would flood the city.

Black was making about the same money dealing with Cameisha but wasn't satisfied. He was too busy counting her money to be content with his own. She was making more than him and he knew it. It was no coincidence that Bad Ass was the last man standing in the trap each night. He had enough work to break Capo and Tamir off thus sealing their allegiance.

Likewise, the supply at his mama's house never ran dry. Never. Mama was picking up and dropping off like Fed-Ex. He knew first hand she was a hustler, and now she was hustling for someone else. Black realized he was quietly being pushed aside. This was his way of pushing back.

"A-yo where my soda?" Self asked through a dense plume of weed smoke. When his eyes lifted from her empty hands, he saw the look on her face and asked, "What's wrong?"

"Call your sister!"

****

"Ceelo!" Aqua shouted when 4, 5, 6 came up on her roll. She and Trigga had been playing every night since she taught him the game. Instead of money, they were betting trips to Mississippi. Trigga was down a whole month when the phone rang.

Meisha twisted her lips at the vibrating phone then glanced at the clock. Since she was in business with the only friends she had, she picked it up. She listened intently with a smile spreading on her face.

"Sho-nuff!" she cheered while Angel repeated the conversation verbatim. The girl had a phonographic memory, which recorded all pauses, commas, and inflections. It was good at times like that but sucked in arguments. She could repeat what you said in so much detail, you couldn't deny it.

"Ok, let me speak to Self," she said once she heard the plan.

"I'm here. You want me to...handle that?" he asked staring into Angel's eyes to make sure she knew what was coming. She knew exactly what he meant and lowered her head in acquiescence. Blood might be thicker than water, but it's not quite as thick as cum.

"You? Nah, we got this. Just do what you been doing," she advised. She knew Self was down with the team but murder was a whole different ball game. Niggas talk that killer shit until it's time to go kill something. "Yes!"

"What?" Trigga asked once she hung up. He had only heard her half of the bizarre conversation and wanted the other half.

"Great new!" she cheered, jumping to her feet and pumping her fist while spinning around. Aqua just shook her head at the antics of her goofy friend. She was acting like she had scored the winning goal.

"What?" he repeated.

"That dude Black is getting ready to rob me. Gonna move up to a key and take it from me!" she barely got past her huge smile.

"And...you're happy about this?" Trigga asked scratching his head.

"Hells yeah! I want that damn apartment complex. That lame is in my way. I would have been wrong if I just killed him for it. Now, I have a reason to body his ass."

"I'll do it," he offered sweetly, proving that chivalry wasn't dead.

"Sure. His sister said he needs a buyer for the brick he's stealing from me. Give him a call."

"What's the number?"

****

"Sup shawty, I need to bump into you today," Black said when Cameisha took his call the next day.

"Okay," she sang sounding giddy. The tone made Black think she was finally about to give in. He had been shooting at her since they began doing business and only got the stiff arm. Usually terse replies to the negative. Never 'okay.'

"Oh! Yeah I um, got a few orders so I'ma need a whole one."

"A whole kilo!" she gushed fanning herself like an old time southern bell. Trigga cracked up when she threw in an "I declare!"

"Sho-nuff, you know a nigga getting his weight up. So get ready cuz I'm finna make you my lady," he said nodding his head to the sound of his macking.

"Tell you what...if we both live to see tomorrow...I'll be your girl," she vowed and hung up.

Black almost had a second thought, but the way his scales were set up... You can't expect a snake to be anything other than a snake.

"My turn," Trigga said and dialed the same number.

"Sup?" Black asked when he took the call from the unknown number.

"What's up Black? This yo' boy...um? TJ," Trigga fumbled. "From College Park? Be with Man 'ndem."

"Oh yeah, yeah, what's poppin' TJ," he replied not letting on that he wasn't sure who it was. He did know a Man 'ndem, but who doesn't? He decided to keep talking and hopefully it would come to him during the conversation.

"Shawty we fucked up out chea! I need a brick; I'll pay thirty for it right now!" Trigga said. He set the ticket so high Black couldn't refuse. Even if he had a buyer for the twenty five thousand kilos were selling for, he would go with the better deal. Real snakes do real snake things.

"Boy I got you! I'ma hit you back when I get straight!"

"Who that? What's going on?" Sparks demanded when Black hung up. He could tell by his elation that it was something good.

"My nigga TJ from College Park. Got twenty for the brick right now," Black hissed. "Shit, fuck cooking and cutting and trappin', we gon' get this quick flip!"

"Twenty bands? We gon' split it fifty-fifty?" Sparks pursed his lips and asked.

"Of course nigga! You my nigga! We gotta shoot that lil' nigga Shawty a rack or two though," he agreed with his slimy ass.

The scumbag deserved everything that was coming his way.

Chapter 14

"What chu making?" Aqua asked like an inquisitive child. She had never known her friend to cook anything other than coke so all the flour in the kitchen called for an investigation.

"I'm making just desserts, also known as scumbag pie," Cameisha replied with a scowl on her face. She continued to weigh out 2.2 pounds of bleached, all-purpose flour with one purpose in mind. Aqua scrunched her face at the odd sound and shook her head "nah."

"I'm good," she proclaimed and popped a frozen Fat-Fat burger in the microwave oven.

"Girl you gonna have a Fat-Fat baby you keep eating all them thangs," she said taking a break from her task. As soon as Cameisha rubbed her belly, the baby moved against her hand. "It moved! Yo it's moving!"

"It's supposed to move. It's a baby duh," Aqua replied as if it was her friend who was a little slow. "When you and Trigga gon' have a baby?"

"Huh? A who? Chile ain't nobody got time for that! We be too busy to be tyrna make a damn baby," she replied with mixed emotions.

"I can tell! The way y'all went at it last night. Oh Trigga, oh Trigga, get it Trigga!" Aqua mocked and cracked up.

"So!" Meisha shot back embarrassed. "Girl it's time for you to get a place. You fucking up my groove!"

She left out the part about her sleeping in the spot of her all-time favorite sexual position, bent over the arm of the sofa. They discovered it quite by accident when they returned after a late night of partying. They were both hot and bothered from the mobile foreplay in the car. Then again in the elevator, hallway, and until they stumbled inside.

There was no way they could make it all the way to the bedroom so he pulled her skirt up and bent her over the arm of the sofa. Trigga entered her so forcefully they both shrieked. A few minutes later, they both howled again from the mutual climax. Best nut she'd ever had but Miss Fat-Fat was in the way of history repeating itself.

"Once this is all over with I'm moving to South America. Me and Trigga gonna have ten kids and live happily ever after!" Cameisha announced wistfully.

Time ceased as she drifted away in those pleasant thoughts. It wouldn't be anything like her own fucked up upbringing as the child of a crack head.

"What?" Aqua smiled along with the content smile on her friend's face. Something she'd never seen before. She had seen her happy before, but never at peace. Never content.

"Nothing," Meisha said snapping out of it. She shook her head wiping the thoughts away like clearing an Etch-a-sketch. It was just wishful thinking because there was no end in sight.

The microwave's ding stole Aqua's already short attention. She juggled the hot burger from hand to hand on her way back to the sofa. Meisha got back to work. She carefully wrapped the flour in the same shape and wrapping as a real kilo. She had just sealed it when Trigga traipsed in.

"Looks good," he nodded approvingly as he handled the fake brick. He picked it up, flipped it over, and asked, "He won't test it?"

"Nah, we did too much business already. That would be suspect as hell. Plus, I be playing the dumb blonde role around them. They dumb enough to believe it. The robber damn sure ain't gon' test it."

"How you know the nigga won't just come in bussing?" he asked.

"Black is a grimy, slimy dude. He thinks he'll be able to rob me, chill for awhile, and then rob me again," she explained. "Plus, I buss back daddy."

"Save him for me. I want this nigga myself," Trigga growled.

"Y'all got some heat?"

"Hell yeah! My nigga Troy done copped us some choppas! Once we try them bitches out on these bitches we gon' be ready to get at Juan 'ndem," he said confidently.

"Ok baby," Cameisha replied pensively. She knew it would take more than a couple of AK-47s to go up against the Columbians.

She thought about calling her uncle Killa for some help.

****

"Say shawty, why don't you take my sister to the movies? Black asked when he came in and found Self and Angel cuddled up on the sofa watching DVDs. "All y'all do is fuck. You need to throw it back too lil' sis."

"Ugh! I hate you!" Angel spat in disgust and stormed upstairs.

"You right. Ain't my sister 'posed to be coming?" Self asked cocking his head.

"Huh? Nah, she um, called and said she can't come till later. Here, y'all go catch a flick. On me," Black said peeling a twenty-dollar bill off a roll of bills. "Get some chips and soda from the gas station cuz it cost too much in the movie."

"That's what's up," Self agreed and took the money. He hopped up the stairs and joined his girl in the room.

"You know why he wants us out of the house don't you?" Angel asked peeling off her skimpy around the house shorts to replace them with some skimpy around town shorts.

"Huh?" he asked since the sight of her in panties stole his sense of hearing.

"My brother. You know he up to something right?" she repeated.

"And you know what comes along with that, don't you?" he replied.

"He already got my mama's house shot up once. Another time some men came in here and held guns on me and my mama 'cause he was playing with they money," Angel pouted.

"Well, you won't have to worry about that no more. Get dressed. I wanna see that "Yung Pimpin'" movie anyway."

"Ok! I heard it was funny!" she smiled and squeezed into the shorts. Once they were changed, they hit the steps to head out.

"You must be hitting that from the back 'cause lil' sis ass getting fat!" Black cheered and high fived Sparks.

"Bye," Angel waved with an air of finality that even he picked up on.

"Damn girl, you act like you moving to another country! I'll see you later!"

"No, you won't," she corrected over her shoulder as they left. She would see him later, but it would be his wake and he would be asleep. She was cool with that.

"I need to get me a car," Self announced as they began the walk to the mall. They had to avoid the shortcuts due to the crispy whiteness of their matching sneakers. Still, it wasn't a long walk, but it was a much shorter drive.

"So get on with some of that money you got stashed under the floorboard in my closet," Angel teased.

"Girl, you done peeped my stash spot!" Self exclaimed.

"Boy stop! I made that spot! My mama smoke dope remember? I been stashing shit since I was eight. Besides, I would guard it with my life. I love you Self."

"...It look like? I think it might rain."

****

Cameisha checked the pistol under the fake kilo for the fifth time as she came to a stop in front of the apartment. It was cocked, locked, and ready to rock just like she was. Instinctively, she scanned her surroundings and processed the information. She noticed Black's Caprice tucked off a few buildings away. Then Shawty rushed by and ducked his head. She couldn't see his face, but the bright red, white, and blue Adidas screamed, "Here's Shawty!" Meisha unbuttoned another button on her shirt and got out.

"Hey y'all," she sang as she stepped inside the apartment. Both men's eyes shot to the tittie meat protruding from the top of her shirt just like she knew they would. She had enough time to draw her gun and kill them both if she chose to, but didn't. She'd promised to save them for Trigga anyway.

"Sup shawty. You brung that?" Black asked when his gaze finally made it up to her face. First, it was the breasts, then down to her crotch, back to her breasts, lips, and finally eyes.

"Shole did," she smiled and batted her eyes. She kept smiling and pretended not to see him press send on his phone. She knew who was getting that text.

"Well let's step into my office," he offered, holding out his arm for her to go first. Black was no gentleman, he just wanted to see that ass. He bit his lip and shook his head as it shook in front of him.

Once they all sat around the shaky old table, Cameisha put both hands in her bag. One came out and placed the coke on the table. The other stayed in the bag gripping the pistol. Cameisha aimed it in the bag, under the table, right between his legs. If shit popped off, he was going to show up on judgment day as a woman. It was obvious by the fake smiles all around that they were all waiting for something. Actually, someone, and there he came.

"Y'allknowwhatthisis!" he shouted barely comprehensible under the bandana tied around his mouth. Even if his eyes, the top of his face, and the grey around the temples didn't tell on him, the bright sneakers once again announced, "Here's Shawty!" Meisha still had to fuck with him.

"Huh? What?" she asked and turned to Black. "What he say?"

The gun, the mask, and coke on the table could only mean one thing, but she played dumb. At the same time, turning the gun on him.

"Isaidya…" Shawty started then paused to lift the bandana from his mouth. Cameisha could have emptied her clip in his face while he fumbled with the mask and shotgun. "I said, y'all break y'all self! Come off that damn key! Fo' I murk y'all!"

Black just shook his head at how badly it was going. Even he knew the robber shouldn't have known the amount of drugs if it wasn't a set up. He looked at Cameisha to see if she caught it, but she was in full dumb blonde mode. Just when it couldn't go any worse, here came his mama. It just got worse.

"Self I need 12 mo'!" Mama Johnson shouted when she bust in the door. Seeing the front room empty, she ran up the steps. "Where you at son-in-law? I need 12 mo'!"

She found her daughter's room empty and rushed back down and walked into what had to be *thee* most comical drug stick up in the entire history of drug stick-ups.

"Hey baby, Sparks, Shawty," she greeted before turning to Cameisha. "Where yo' lil' brother at? I need 12 for the fiddy."

"Um…he's not here. We're kinda in the middle of something," she replied hoping to get on with the robbery. If it went south, she would have murdered everyone in the room. She liked Angel and all but Mama would have to go. She was young; she'd get over it.

"Yeah Mama, come back later and I'll take care of you," Black gently urged. Mama Johnson twisted her lips dubiously because her son never gave her that deal. Still, she turned on her heels to catch Bad Ass in the trap knowing he would.

"Um…where were we?" Meisha asked hopefully.

"Um? Oh! The kilo, gimme that damn brick," Shawty demanded. He snatched it off the table and looked to Black to see what he wanted to do next. Black pointed to the back door with his eyes sending him on his way.

"Oh my God! We got robbed!" Meisha let out a phony wail and fanned herself with her hand. "I do declare!"

"We 'bout to find out who that was! We 'bout to straighten this! Come on Sparks," Black shouted. His acting chops were so good that Cameisha nearly clapped.

"Be careful!" she yelled after them as they rushed out of the apartment. Once they were gone, she pulled her phone out to call Trigga. "You're up next!"

Chapter 15

Cameisha wasn't the only one dialing Trigga's phone. Black hadn't even made it to his car before he did the same, with his thirsty ass. "TJ? This Black, you ready?"

"Yeah come on. You know the New World car wash on Godby Road?" Trigga asked setting the trap.

"Yeah I know where you talking 'bout. I need to wash my donk anyway. 'Bout an hour?"

"That's what's up. What you pushing?" Trigga asked.

"A Chevy sitting on 30s," he said proudly. It was proof that somewhere along the way black people got life fucked up. Who gives a fuck about how big your rims are? Do women say 'oh he has big rims; he'll be a good provider"? Probably not, but police will pull you over every chance they get.

"An hour," Trigga repeated and hung up. He turned to his right hand man seated on his right hand and asked, "You ready?"

Troy twisted his lips like 'yeah right' and chambered one of the fifty 7.62 rounds into the chamber. Trigga smiled at the sound of the chopper and cocked his as well. They loaded the guns into the van they'd rented from a junkie. Inside were coveralls used by both painters and hit men. Pretty much for the same reason. Paint or blood, no one wants it on their clothes.

****

"Let me ride with y'all," Shawty pleaded when Black came to get the stolen kilo of cocaine.

"Nah, my nigga TJ ain't tryna meet no new people, you feel me," he explained. It sounded reasonable so Shawty twisted his lips in acceptance. "Don't worry Shawty, I got you a rack for helping out, plus we finna ball out in the club tonight."

"Turn up?" he asked hopefully. He had heard everyone talking about turning up but never got to actually turn up himself. It's not much of a consolation, but he was about to turn up dead for the robbery.

"Hell yeah! Turn up, ball out, all that," Black cheered. The smile that spread on his face meant he went for it. He handed the fake dope over and sat down to wait. Good thing he didn't decide to hold his breath.

"Surprised that nigga ain't try to come with us," Sparks said when Black returned to the car.

"You know he did," he laughed as he put the kilo under his seat. "I told him we was hitting the club tonight."

There would be no tonight or tomorrow for those two. The music blasting through the car was their going away party. The blunt they smoked was their one for the road. After that day, people would pour out a little liquor for them and speak of them in the past tense.

Trigga and Troy parked across from the ambush spot and waited. They chose that car wash because you couldn't drive through. Once you pulled in, you were stuck.

"That them?" Troy asked when the Chevy pulled in. It was a rhetorical question so Trigga didn't bother to answer. He put the van in drive and crept across the street.

"Car wash? Five bucks!" an industrious junkie announced when Black pulled in.

"Why not? Still got fifteen minutes," Black miscalculated. He had two or three minutes tops left in life. He backed into the stall and the junkie got to work.

No sooner did he begin spraying the car, did the van pull up and block the exit. When the side door popped open, he had seen enough. Trigga and Troy jumped out as he scurried behind the car.

"What the..." was all Sparks got out before shots rang out. He lifted his arms to block the shots and quickly realized the fallacy in that. The huge slugs blew chunks of meat and bone from his forearms. When he dropped them, the bullets slammed into his head and chest making him a memory.

Black ducked down flat to escape the flurry of death crashing through the car. There was a brief pause and he made a dash. As soon as he opened his door, the firing began again. The bullets easily passed through the car door and knocked him down. Trigga walked forward letting off single shots.

"Hey man!" the junkie complained when Black picked him up to use as a shield. The bullets easily passed through his emaciated body and dropped Black again.

"Wait! Wait! I got a whole brick in my car. You can have it!" Black pleaded.

"Keep it!" Trigga barked and tugged on the trigger. Two rounds literally tore the top of his head off answering the question of if he actually had a brain or not.

"Let's ride!" Troy yelled and jumped back in the van. Trigga was right behind him and pulled off. Once they safely made it to the highway, he pulled out his phone.

"Done deal," Trigga reported proudly when Meisha picked up.

"All three of them?" she asked hopefully.

"You mean three as in the junkie that got caught up or was it 'posed to be three in the car?" he asked even though he knew the answer.

"Aw man," she pouted and hung up. On cue, Bad Ass came in from the trap to put the money up and empty his bladder. "A-yo, you seen that nigga Shawty out there?" she asked.

"Just seen the clown," Bad Ass snarled twisting his face up. He felt some kind of way about getting knocked out and not being able to get some get back.

"Here," Cameisha said extending her pistol.

"What's this for?" he asked just to be certain.

"Time for you to bust your cherry. Time for you to get your dick wet!"

****

Self, Bad Ass, Angel, and Leera sat around smoking blunts while a DVD played. Only the girls paid attention because the boys had murder on their minds. Self knew Black was deceased so he waited for the official news to comfort his girl. The fact that it happened across town shifted suspicion from them. The fake kilo the police found allowed them to sweep it under the rug as drug related.

Meanwhile Bad Ass was mentally preparing to kill for the first time in his young life. Bust his cherry. Since Black wasn't around to feed the trappers, he knew the trap would be slow. That was when he would make his move. He was a little antsy about it, but nothing more. He couldn't wait to murder Shawty.

"Ugh! Let's go upstairs!" Angel hissed when Leera ducked under a blanket on Bad Ass' lap.

"Ugh nothing. You better stop being scared to suck dick! How you 'posed to keep a man if you don't suck no dick?" she shot back. It sounded good in theory but in reality, she sucked plenty of dicks and still couldn't keep a man. They'd had that same debate so many times that Angel refused to go there again. "If you won't, someone else will!"

"Whatever. If he wants some head he can go get some," she said pulling Self upstairs.

"You know..."

"Shut it! Zip!" Angel demanded knowing he was about to side with her friend. She was far too high and horny to argue so she began to strip. Getting naked must be contagious because Self quickly followed suit. Once they reached their birthday suits, they climbed in bed and had sex for the third time that day.

"Man, I told you not to cum in my mouth," Leera moaned once Bad Ass did just that. She really didn't mind.

"Uh..." he replied not knowing what to say. And really, what was there to say? How can a woman suck, kiss, lick, and stroke a man's penis and expect him to say 'stop', wait, I'm about to cum? Not going to happen.

"Your turn," she said, trying him.

He frowned thinking about how much her name got tossed around the trap. Seemed every one of the trappers tossed her up. Meanwhile, none of them got close to Angel.

"Not today," he declined like he did the day before and would do the next day. She twisted her lips as he rolled a condom on then assumed the position. Once Bad Ass entered her doggy style, he humped her hard and fast like a doggy does.

The sounds of sex echoed throughout the otherwise quiet apartment. Splashing, skin smacking, shit talking, and moans reverberated in the air. That was followed by the grunt of a good nut and the soft snores that follow a good nut. A couple of hours later both Self and Bad Ass popped up as if synchronized.

"You ready?" Self whispered when he met Bad Ass in the kitchen.

"Fuck yeah, that nigga snuffed me," he whispered back and made sure a round was in the chamber.

"Want me to come?"

"Nah, stay here," Bad Ass replied and slid out the back door. He slowly began to creep towards the back of the complex where Shawty lived with his mother. Actually, he lived in the unfinished basement with a lock on the door preventing him from stealing anything else. He wasn't the only one creeping.

"What y'all doing?" Leera whispered when she snuck up on Self in the kitchen. He was startled by her voice and spun on his heels. Got startled again when he saw Leera was naked.

"Huh?" was all that would come out. For a reply, she dropped in front of him and went for his zipper. "W...wh...what are you...oh!"

He got it real quick when he entered her hot mouth. Instead of looking out for his partner, he watched her blow him. While she was sucking him, Shawty was sucking on a glass dick. He loaded a rock on his shooter and took a long sizzling pull.

"Mmm," both Leera and Shawty moaned as their sucking paid off. She got a mouthful of cum while he filled his lungs with crack smoke. She swallowed, stood, and walked off. He wondered who the fuck was tapping on his door that time of night. Hoping they had more dope, he went to investigate.

"Who?" Shawty demanded. He was hot about having to release the hit from his lungs sooner than planned. A veteran crack head can hold a hit for up to seven minutes. They would make great pearl divers if they weren't crack heads.

Bad Ass ignored the question and tapped again. His heart began to pound in his ears when he heard Shawty opening the door. He lifted the gun, closed his eyes, and fired twice. When he opened them, Shawty was staring back in shock.

"You...tried to shoot me?" he asked in disbelief. That time Bad Ass took aim and fired into his face. The shot dropped him in the doorway so he shot him again and took off.

Self was watching Leera play in her pussy when he heard footsteps coming fast. A second later Bad Ass rushed inside breathing heavily.

"I did that shit son! Knocked that nigga's block off!" he whispered loudly.

"Sh!" Self warned knowing Leera was awake. She had just proved to him two things at once. One, she could not be trusted and two, she had some good ass head.

Chapter 16

"You have been ducking me!" Anna bellowed when she finally caught up with her cousin at his condo.

"Obviously not well enough," he shot back and shot Manny a cross look for letting her in. He shrugged helplessly and slinked away. "Now that you have tracked me down, what do you want?"

"Have you spoken to Mama Salazar?" she began. The secret of his sister was on the tip of her tongue waiting to escape.

"Por que?" he frowned meaning he hadn't. "What do you want? Another hand out? The family is on the verge of war and you have your hand out! Another car? Money?"

"I..."

"You are selfish! They say the product is dangerous? Well fix it! Here!" he yelled thrusting a kilo of cocaine at her. He scrambled through his bag and came up with a CD containing Samantha's formula. "If you're not with us, you're against us!"

"Si, I..." was all Anna could get out before Juan stormed off. He was plenty mad but part of the rush was some good white girl head across town. He had moved Samantha up to the master bedroom. She was still under guard and without communication, but Juan was spending all of his spare time over there.

Anna looked at the brick of pure cocaine in one hand and the CD containing the formula in the other. It was true that she could get anything she wanted from her drug dealing clan. If she could help them in return she would. Maybe it would prevent more dead bodies from filling the morgue. She put them in her purse and left right behind her cousin.

****

"Think there's drugs in her bag?" Brice asked as he and Toshiba watched Anna come out of the condo they had been staking out. They both knew Juan wouldn't have anything on him. The shell game of multiple stops at multiple houses made him hard to follow.

"And if she does have some? Possession, probation, slap on the wrist. I want the big fish," she supervised from the passenger seat. "You like?" she laughed when Anna bent over her trunk. The move stretched her tight skirt against her round Columbian ass showing she was partial to French cut panties.

"It's a'ight, not as nice as yours," Brice chuckled. The compliment was meant as a joke even though the younger man and older lady would eventually fuck if they kept spending so much time together. His mind flashed to Cameisha for a second. That was the tail he really wanted to tail.

"Well, let's follow her anyway so we can make our report," she sighed. Part of their detail was to follow the boring girl once a week. She went to work, home, church, and to see family. Totally predictable.

****

"Remarkable!" Anna remarked as she read the formula on her computer. She tried to hate on her discovery but it was brilliant. "I have to try this! I'll reduce the electrons and maybe, just maybe..."

The very bright girl realized it would be very dumb to try to use the lab at work. Instead, she hit the supply closet and loaded up on equipment. Beakers, burners, and assorted items went in a box. After loading the borrowed equipment in her car, she went back and got Harry. Harry was the resident lab rat who worked as a guinea pig.

Anna started with a gram and ended with four. She prayed a little prayer before injecting a rat sized dose in Harry's leg. If rats can smile, that's what he did before jumping on his little wheel. He ran for a while then got off and stared up at Anna for another hit like a little junkie.

"I think we have something!" she cheered and got back to work. By the end of the night, she had four kilos of synthetic coke. "Now what?"

****

Anna wasn't the only one playing with drugs. Lisa pulled out the package of heroin daily and pushed it around with her fingernail. That went on for a week before she finally took a taste. Literally, at first, as she licked the bitter powder. That taste sped through every cell in her body and activated her addition. She used that same manicured nail to scoop a hit of Boy into each nostril.

"Oh boy!" she applauded as that old feeling came back. She went into a nod right there on the toilet. That was exactly how Dasia found her.

"Girl I know you heard me...you ok?" she asked confused by the curious angle.

"Mm, better than ever!" Lisa gushed. To prove it, she dipped between Dasia's legs and ate her better than ever.

****

That was life for Dasia and Lisa. One big party, turn down for what? Like they say, it ain't tricking if it's stolen. The condo was full of different people all day and most nights. Rita and Tina popped through daily to smoke, snort, and steal as much as they could.

In the beginning, Dasia would pull an ounce a day from one of the two remaining kilos. Some days two, weekends even more. A cloud of weed smoke perpetually hung in the air like Beijing smog.

Nightly orgies became the order of the day. The libations fed libidos, which led to licentiousness. Cash Money would pop through from time to time to discreetly serve Lisa the heroin she was using more and more often. He or any other guys would be treated to blow jobs or pony rides by Rita or Tina. Dasia felt a stab of heterosexuality watching

Tina slowly ride him on the sofa. For the first time in a long time, she craved some dick.

Yup, one big party. The girls maxed out the thousand dollar daily limit at the ATM every day. They ate, shopped, and partied like there was no tomorrow. The irony was that if you live life at that speed there won't be a tomorrow. It couldn't last; any day could be your last.

Yup, all bad until it got worse. Lisa hid her heroin use from Dasia as best as she could. She started off small by mixing the coke and heroin together in what's known as a speedball. The volatile combination wreaks havoc on the brain as it pushes and pulls at the same time. It's the same shit that killed John Belushi, River Phoenix, and a bunch of other people you've never heard of. Dasia stumbled across her new addiction quite by accident.

"Li-Li! All that gone from yesterday?" Dasia called out to Lisa in the shower. She'd pulled two ounces of coke out just the night before and couldn't find a trace of it. She looked everywhere except in Rita's purse, which is where it was. She'd cuffed it that morning before she went home.

"In the living room!" Lisa yelled from under the water and steam.

"I'm in the living room," Dasia muttered to herself. A crystal candy jar that used to hold the coke sat empty on the glass table. Lisa's purse was open on the sofa so Dasia checked there. "Here we go!"

The coke had an odd texture to it but it wasn't the time to try to analyze. It was time to get high. She lit a blunt and took a hearty pull as she fixed two long lines to start the day off with.

"Oh my!" Dasia grimaced curiously when she inhaled the first line. She could tell immediately that something was different. What, she wasn't sure so she leaned in and snorted the remaining line.

Ask any addict who is addicted to anything how they got hooked and most will tell you it was because of that first hit. That first blast of euphoria that they will never, ever, no matter how much you smoke, snort, or shoot, be able to duplicate. Most will spend the rest of their junkie careers pursing what they can't catch. Chasing the dragon. Stalking a lie, they held as a truth.

"Mm," she moaned as they life-altering chemicals sped through her system. She swayed gently to the sexy music playing in her mind and leaned into her first nod.

"Oh no!" Lisa said when she came in and found Dasia in the obtuse angle. Her eyes shot to her open purse, the open package, and then back to her lover. The moment of dread passed and morphed into relief. She would no longer have to hide. She spilled some of the dope on the table and lined it up.

After she inhaled them both, she joined Dasia in a nod.

Chapter 17

With Black now permanently in the past tense Cameisha was officially the man in Eastwyck. She directly supplied the trappers. The introduction of the good dope caused an influx of new customers. Crack heads from all over Decatur were finding out about the glass being sold on Candler Road. That was quickly going to become a problem because the supply was running out.

Trigga kept his word about locking down the west side of Atlanta. Westfield and Oak Tree Apartments exclusively sold his dope. The mid-level dealers felt the pinch and came to him to supply them too, but he too was running out of dope. The only thing worse than not having enough customers is having enough customers but not enough dope. He came home with sixty thousand dope dollars hoping to buy three kilos from Cameisha.

"No can do," Cameisha said firmly when he rushed into the kitchen while she was cooking crack. She even shook her head 'no' so there would be no misunderstanding. Or so you would think.

"What do you mean no?" he whined like a five year old being denied a juice box. He had one kilo left and it would not last.

"No. It's an adjective. Used elliptically as a slogan, notice, etc. To forbid, reject, deny, or deplore a thing specified," she replied sarcastically, with her smart ass. She could hear music from "Jeopardy" coming out of his ears as he tried to translate what she'd said. He cocked his head curiously like a puppy does. "No means no babe. I ain't got it. I'm at the end of the road!"

"Shit. I hate to have to whip this last one! I don't wanna lose my new constituency," he grumbled.

"Constituency! My baby been watching CNN!" she teased.

"Nah, my nigga Verb said it in a song. Real talk, we need a connect shawty!"

99

"I know, I know," she said racking her brain for a source. She ran through her mental rolodex searching names and faces until she struck gold. "Oh, oh! I know who!"

"Who?" Trigga yelled behind her as she took off out of the kitchen. She ran into the living room and grabbed their photo album.

"Yo, 'member that couple we met down in Belize? They had the little boy?" she asking fingering through the pictures.

"Yeah? Yeah! They said the hotel dude had that work!" he shouted joining her jubilee.

"That's right!" Meisha shouted as she checked the book. When she finally found the number, she held it high like the Olympic torch.

****

"Ramel! A-yo Ra! You better come get your son before I choke his little ass out!" Andrea screamed at the top of her lungs.

"What now?" Ra laughed as he came into the bedroom to investigate. Knowing their son, it could be absolutely anything. The gorgeous child shared their good looks but had absolutely no chill. The boy was prone to say exactly what was on his mind. No matter how much trouble he got in for it.

"This dude gon' tell me I need to put his sister back where I got her from! Talking 'bout she cry too much! I should give him something to cry about," she yelled. She was talking to Ra but staring down at Ra Junior as she spoke. The boy shrugged his shoulders like 'oh well' and walked off.

"What I wanna know is how come every time you mad at him he's my son? When he's good, he's your little man, bad, my son. Riddle me that?" Ra asked twisting his lips.

"Whatever, get your daughter. She's wet," Dre laughed and walked off.

"And every time she's wet she's my daughter," Ra grumbled as he went to scoop the baby out of her crib. She had been fussing about being wet but snapped out of it when she saw her daddy. She smiled, cooed, and kicked her little legs in excitement. Daddies are kids' first rock stars. How in the world do they leave them?

"Come on lil' mama," Ra sang as he picked the baby up. Andrea's phone began to ring and she came to answer it.

"Yeah!" Dre barked into the phone like people do when it's an unknown number. If the number isn't assigned to a name, it could be anybody.

"Hello, um? I'm tryna reach Andrea?" Cameisha replied tentatively.

"Who dis?" Dre barked frowning up as if the caller could see her.

"Um, my name is Cameisha. I met her down in Belize, we..."

"Oh hey girl," she sang turning into sista gurl. "How you doing honey chile?"

"Good, good. I um, I need to holla at you 'bout some business. Can we meet?"

"Sure. It's daddy's day with the kids so I'm free," she said making it daddy's day with the kids. She mean-mugged Ra daring him to deny it.

Ramel didn't even flinch. He had no problem spending the day with his children. He had been so busy doing what he does, but that's Stud 5.

"Meet me at the Halal restaurant on Piedmont. We can have lunch on the patio," Dre suggested eagerly.

"Can't wait!" Meisha shot back just as willing.

****

"That's what's up," Trigga responded when Cameisha announced her lunch plans. "You taking shawty with you?"

"Yeah, we going to look at an apartment over there on Candler. Somewhere close so I can check on her every day," she said, proving she planned to be on the east side every day.

"Can't wait to get my sofa back," he slyly suggested causing his woman to blush.

"Me too!" she giggled. They traded a couple of pecks on the lips before Trigga departed. As soon as he got down to his car, he pulled his phone to call his right hand man.

"Sup shawty," Troy answered sounding extremely relaxed. He should, because what's more relaxing than some good old, southern head? Nothing, that's what.

"Huh?" Shawna asked pausing the blowjob thinking he was talking to her.

"Not you shawty. You keep doing what you doing," he said guiding himself back inside the comfy confines of her jaws.

"See you putting that deadly dick on another one. Just don't kill her," Trigga laughed at the exchange.

"That ain't even funny shawty," he said feeling wounded. He felt some kinda way about Ta-Ta dying on him but news of Samantha's murder had him hot. He wanted to kill Juan himself for that.

"Anyway, I'm on my way. Be there in a few minutes."

"Hurr up, these niggas is thirsty!" Troy exclaimed and clicked off. Just in time because a second later he filled Shawna's mouth with babies. She obviously was thirsty too and swallowed every drop.

"You got some powder?" Shawna asked making it sound like a favor and not payment for the blowjob.

"Shole do," he replied and gladly parted with a gram of the powdered cocaine. He carried several gram packages for situations like that.

The packages should be called 'Crack Head Starter Kits' because that's exactly what they were. Ask any junkie how they got on the hard and most will tell you that they started with the soft. Dig a little deeper and you'll find some marijuana was the gateway. Harmless weed huh? That's how Shawna's own mother got started many years earlier. Now she was on the opposite side of the complex sucking dick for rocks at that same moment.

****

"Hey girl! You look so different!" Cameisha gushed when she met Andrea on the restaurant patio. She stood and they embraced warmly.

"Girl that's because I had a person inside of me," Dre laughed.

"That's right, what you have?"

"A diva. Now I have a matching set so I'm done," she said trying to convince herself. "Who's your friend?"

"Oh my bad. This is my girl Aqua. Aqua, Andrea," she said making the belated introductions.

"Hello Aqua. What you got there?" Dre smile and patted Aqua's belly. Aqua had her arms crossed and lip poked out.

"Duh, it's a baby," she shot back curtly and turned her head like a truculent child.

"Um...ok, I'm sorry," Dre said gently. She knew firsthand the emotional roller coaster that is pregnancy.

"Don't pay her any mind. She mad 'cause they wouldn't let her bring her Fat-Fat burgers in," Meisha explained with a laugh.

"I have no idea what that means, but they make the best turkey burgers on the planet," Dre offered. By the time, she finished laying out the ingredients and etcetera's; Aqua was smiling and nodding in agreement.

They all took seats on the patio and made congenial small talk until the food arrived. Once Aqua got settled into her new favorite food, Cameisha got down to business.

"Yo, I need some work. I need to get plugged in with that dude from the hotel in Belize," she admitted.

"Hold on one second," Dre said holding up a finger and pulling out her phone. "Bae, you owe me a grand!"

"What was that about?" Cameisha laughed when she hung up.

"Oh, I bet my husband why you called. He said it was personal. I bet it was business. I won."

"Now I feel bad! I been meaning to call since we got back but things been crazy! I'm talkin'..."

"No need to apologize. Trust me, I understand. I used to be you ma," Dre assured her. "My plug in New York is on hold due to a...situation. You gonna have to go straight to the source. That a good news bad news type of deal."

"Start with the good please," Meisha said bracing herself.

"Well the good news is the price. We were only paying five grand each when we dealt with him. The bad news is you gotta get them shits back stateside yourself. And that is serious business!"

"So how you get them back?" Cameisha almost demanded. She caught her tone and adjusted accordingly. "I mean, I can do what y'all did."

"Nah, someone snitched on our mule. Now I don't know if she gon' stand up or lay down," Andrea replied twisting her lips in thought.

"Shit for five thou apiece I'ma find a way! Tell dude we on our way!" Cameisha shouted.

Dre made a coded call to Belize and told Rude Boy that she recommended his hotel. That was all that would be said over the phone. The mood went back to friendly girl talk as Aqua smashed turkey burgers piled high with fixings.

"I'ma need some of these to go please!" Aqua announced with a full mouth.

****

"Welp, this the last one," Trigga informed his partner when he broke out the last kilo.

"Shit, we need a plug! We gotta get on ASAP! 'Specially if we gon' hit the niggas in Glen Valley Apartments off," Troy retorted. "I got some cousins down in that seaport. We may have to make us a trip to Savanah."

"Real spit shawty, after yo' uncle, I really ain't tryna deal with no mo' of yo' family," Trigga teased with a straight face.

"Oh yeah 'cause Dirty-D wasn't nothing like yo' brother Keith!" Troy shot back. Loyalty is thicker than blood and each had killed the other's blood relative to prove it.

"Anyway, my girl got something in the works. If this pop off we gon' be straighter than straight!" Trigga said proudly.

"Good! So let's hit Glen Valley first. Get them niggas straight and lay out the rules."

"You trust them?" Trigga asked raising his eyebrows so he could hear the answer.

"Nope. That's why I'm bringing you two," Troy replied pointing at the shotgun leaning in the corner. Troy separated ten G-packs for the new workers and Trigga grabbed the gun. They bent a few corners before Troy pulled into yet another crime and drug infested ghetto apartment complex. The junkies from there had been making the trek for the good dope but that brought attention. Attention brings heat and heat brings indictments.

"Must be the trap," Trigga said seeing obvious drug activity in the rear of the complex.

"Hey now!" Troy smiled at the flock of local hoes jocking them as they drove in. He had already run through the whole Oak Tree crew.

"Careful y'all, he got a deadly dick!" Trigga called out as they drove past. Troy just shook his head at his friend's antics.

"Y'all ready to get this bread?" Troy asked as he pulled to a stop at the trap.

"Hell ye...sup shawty?" Rell said stopping short when he saw the shotgun laying across Trigga's lap. To make matters worse, Trigga stared off while patting and petting the gun like a rich chick does with one of those loud ass little lap dogs.

"Don't pay no attention to them. They only speak if money comes short. Now y'all line up and get this work," he answered.

Troy passed out the G-packs and Trigga snapped a picture of every-one who got one. Some frowned inquisitively but said nothing about the pictures. Fuck it; they were getting some work so they could eat, smoke, and fuck. Not Marco though, he had to be the one.

"What are the pictures for shawty?" he asked Trigga who respond-ed by turning his head. A few who wondered the same thing leaned in to hear the reply.

"That's for your people to put by the casket, 'cause I swear to God if anyone comes short, I'm talking one penny short, this the last time they gon' look like they do today!" Troy vowed.

"$750 huh? That's what's up. $750 ain't shit. Shit, I could pay fo' mine now," a shifty eyed teen called Snake rambled when it was time to get his package. He looked at Troy, the dope, the gun, Trigga, the back-seat, floorboard, headliner, look, look, look.

"He gon' be the one," Trigga finally spoke. He talked of the kid's im-pending murder like he wasn't even there.

"Fo' sure," Troy agreed. They knew full well that at least one of the dope boys was going to fuck up. And they were going to get fucked up for it. There was always one. Always.

"Look at it as an investment. He can be a lesson for the others," Trigga sighed. Snake wouldn't learn from it though, dead is dead.

Once the dope boys wrapped up in Glen Valley, they hit off the workers in Oak Tree and finally their alma mater, Westfield. They part-ed ways with a pound and Trigga rushed home to see if Cameisha came up on anything. You already know Troy rushed back over to Glen Val-ley and scooped the head hoe in charge. Same corner store, same cheap malt liquor, cheap motel, and cheap sex with a cheap chick.

"Well? How'd it go? We on?" Trigga asked at a hundred miles an hour when he got home.

"A-yo, pack a bag! We're going to Belize!" she shot back.

"Belize? When?" he asked instead of packing and got scolded.

"Now! Right now, now get packed!"

Chapter 18

'Hoes ain't shit but bitches and tricks. Only good for fucking and sucking dicks!'

"Trigga! Ugh! Turn that moron off!" Cameisha shouted. She didn't wait for him to comply and reached over to turn the car radio off herself. If the song wasn't bad enough on its own, Trigga had been rapping along with it.

"What? You don't fuck with Verb? He's the hottest rapper in the game!" Trigga laughed in his defense.

"Dumbest rapper in the game! I can't with that dude. That song hurts my soul," she said dramatically clutching her chest. "He gave an interview saying he's the new God and he 'bout to write a new bible!"

"Damn, I ain't know he was doing it like that," he replied. Trigga might not have been the brightest or most religious, but was offended by the blasphemy nonetheless. As he should be.

"Boy I'ma set the block on fire with twenty keys!" Cameisha cheered, rubbing her hands together like a mad scientist.

"Um...ten keys," Trigga interjected as a reminder that half of the hundred grand in the suitcase was his. It didn't make them partners, per se, but it was a joint venture.

"Oh, yeah," she replied with a forced smirk. She would much rather run the show completely. Still, ten kilos each represented a million dollars in their household.

The rest of the ride to the airport was made in quiet contemplation. Trigga parked in the long-term lot and led the way into the airport. The couple then scanned the airline signs looking for a flight to Belize. They say proper preparation prevents poor performance so this last minute, off the cuff mission, was doomed from the start.

"Oh, I know!" Cameisha said suddenly and popped herself on the head like she should have had a V-8. She pulled out her phone and hopped on the internet. "Ok, Atlanta to Belize...roundtrip...leaving to-day...tomorrow."

"Tomorrow? Shit, we need to come back tonight!" Trigga ex-claimed as she entered their parameters into the phone.

"Ok, let's see," she said taking his dumbass suggestion. And flying to Belize and returning the same day with twenty kilos is a dumbass sug-gestion indeed. "Nah, gotta be tomorrow."

Mistake number one was booking a one day trip to the Caribbean. Who does that but a drug trafficker? If you were balling hard enough to just fly to Belize for a night, you'd take your own plane to do it. Mistake number two was paying the two-thousand dollar fare in cash.

"One minute please," the pretty clerk smiled as she handled the transaction. The keyboard clicked from her rapid input of data so they had no way of knowing she entered the code for suspected drug activity. At the same time the tickets printed, photos were taken, and a file cre-ated. Various law enforcement agencies would receive the file to check against their open investigations. Cameisha and Trigga were now on the radar.

"She liked me," Trigga joked as they walked away with their tickets.

"That's because you're so pretty," she teased back and cackled like an old witch. That set off one of the famous sessions of playing the dozens. Everyone on the shuttle tram was treated to a comedy show as they went back and forth cracking on each other.

"Your ears so big you can hear into the future," Trigga snapped.

"Nigga your head so big you make a solar eclipse!" she shot back. Back and forth until they reached their terminal. Cameisha got sud-denly sullen once they reached the gate.

"Don't be scared shawty, I'm here," he said misunderstanding her apprehension.

"Scared! I...oh, ok baby," she said taking him up on the offer of his outstretched hand. They interlocked fingers and found their seats. As soon as the plane was airborne, she conked out on his shoulder.

****

"We here bae," Trigga said, gently waking Cameisha as the plane landed in Central America.

"My bad," Meisha giggled and wiped the puddle of slobber she left on his shirt.

"No problem, I been knew you were a drooler!" he laughed setting off round two of jokes.

Once they collected their bags, they walked through the terminal to catch a cab but didn't make it.

"You think he means us?" Trigga asked with trepidation when he saw a bearded man holding a sign.

"Man it's a good thing you're pretty!" Meisha chided and marched straight to the man with their names on his sign. "Who's you?" she demanded like a tough guy.

"You must be them, come on," Malik laughed and turned to lead the way out of the terminal. "Dre asked me to drop you off at the hotel. Call me Unc."

"Oh, ok," Cameisha beamed and extended her bag towards him.

"Yeah right," Malik cracked up and kept walking.

"Bae, you dropped something," Trigga warned pointing at her feet.

"What?" she asked looking down and not seeing anything.

"Your face!" he laughed and set off round three. Malik just shook his head as they cracked on each other all the way to his truck.

"You live down here Unc?" Trigga asked in astonishment as they rode along the magnificent countryside. Even at night, it was brighter than the bleak ghetto of southwest Atlanta. He couldn't fathom people actually lived in such serenity.

"Yeah, I do," Malik nodded in satisfaction. After 40 plus years of the concrete jungle of New York, he was grateful to be there.

"We moving to South America. My people got land down there! We're building houses and everything. We gon' move there and live happily ever after," Meisha said as if trying to convince herself.

"That's nice," Unc replied pensively. He knew firsthand how hard 'happily ever afters' are to come by. He'd been with a hundred women before finding the one. Been in drug deals, shootouts, hospitals, and prisons trying to achieve his happily ever after.

Happily ever afters are doable but a lot more work than most can manage. Most who try to purchase it with drug money go to jail or die trying. He didn't believe in luck so he was grateful to his Lord instead.

"You coming to take us back tomorrow?" Meisha asked when he pulled to a stop in front of the hotel.

"Tomorrow! Are you sure you know what you're doing?" Malik asked Trigga. He shook his head when Trigga's blank expression said they didn't have a clue. "Nah, catch a cab. Go check in and meet Rude Boy at ten. In the bar."

"Welp, we got an hour," Cameisha offered when they checked into their room. That was plenty of time since they stripped immediately. She was as wet as he was hard when they met in the middle of the bed.

"Grr," Trigga growled as he pushed inside of her. Good pussy is definitely something to growl about. You really think Tony the Tiger was happy about some cereal?

Cameisha was so worked up from excitement that she came almost instantly. She braced herself when he scooped her legs onto his shoulders and dove deep. It wasn't long before he bust a nut of his own and collapsed on top of her. The couple basked in the afterglow for a few minutes before hitting the shower. They washed, dried, dressed, and then hit the bar.

"Welcome to the Seaside Hotel!" Rude Boy greeted from behind the bar. He might have owned the joint, but he still worked as a bellhop, cook, waiter, or bartender.

"You must be Rude Boy," Trigga replied, remembering him from their last visit there.

"That's me. My friends Ra and Dre told me to take care of you guys," he said. It was a tacit clarification that they had been vouched for.

"They did," Cameisha nodded explaining that she understood. If she screwed up it would be on Ra and Dre as well.

"We can speak in my office. Jane, watch the bar," he said coming out from around the bar.

"Sure!" Jane cheered since she was actually a guest. Her first duty was fixing herself a double on the house.

"In here," Rude Boy announced as he opened his office door. He stepped aside and took a glance at Cameisha's ass as well as the bag in Trigga's hand. Both made him nod in approval. Once they were seated on opposite sides of a mahogany desk, they got down to business.

"We heard the ticket was five bands?" Trigga began hopefully. A five thousand dollar price tag on a whole kilo was too good to be true. Actually, it was too good to be true.

"Was, it's ten grand now. I lost my mule so the price went up to compensate. Our mutual friend worked for that price and so can you," Rude Boy explained and read the body language.

"Shit we don't mind working! What we gotta do?" Meisha cheered. The dred twisted his mouth in contemplation, and then shook his head no.

"Tell you what, see how this goes, and come back," he decided.

"Well here's a buck," Trigga said placing the hundred thousand on the desk.

"Great. I'll give it to you before you leave. You guys going to the Keys?" Rude Boy asked slipping back into tour guide mode.

"Nah, we leaving tomorrow," Trigga replied.

"Tomorrow!" Rude Boy yelled. "...Remember, you were referred."

****

The sex the next morning was fast, furious, and selfish. Each was focused on busting a nut to ease their minds instead of libido. Cameisha barely got hers off before Trigga grunted and seized in the spasm of a good orgasm.

After relieving themselves, they met in the shower. They thoughtfully washed each other and got out. When they went back into the room, ten kilos sat on the table. They both stared at them like they were afraid of them. Shit had just gotten real.

"Let's get this money!" the dope boy said snapping out of his trance. It was every dope boy's dream, picking up work across the water. He pulled the first layer of clothing out of the suitcase and carefully laid the bricks.

Meisha raised an eyebrow at how inept their plan was. If cocaine smuggling was as easy as just putting bricks in a bag then everybody would be doing it. She was too greedy not to try it so she shrugged her shoulders and said, "I'll get a cab."

'Get greedy, go to jail,' Daddy reminded in reminiscence. The girl caught an attitude with the memory and pursed her lips like a spoiled brat.

****

"Welcome to Belize Air," another pretty clerk said flashing her pretty Caribbean smile and accent.

"Sup," Cameisha huffed as she handed over the tickets. The woman entered the names and frowned at what she read. She glanced up to see Cameisha gawking while Trigga watched a plane take off.

"One second," she offered with another smile but it was less genial than the last. Forced even. She quickly tapped out an alert that the couple was returning. The boarding passes came out of the printer and she handed them over. "Enjoy your flight."

"Un huh," Meisha said cynically as she took them. Poor Trigga, it is a good thing that he's pretty because he missed everything.

'If something feels like it ain't right, it ain't right!'

"I know Daddy, dang!" she pouted.

"Huh? I ain't even say anything," Trigga replied confused by her sudden outburst.

****

"Lookie, lookie, lookie at who it is!" Detective Walton sang as he looked at Cameisha and Trigga's pictures on the latest alert.

"That's the girl!" Brice cheered pointing at the picture, "Belize?"

"Roundtrip to Belize in 24 hours. Way too sloppy for a Salazar associate," Walton said scratching his chin thoughtfully.

"Well she hasn't been seen around the clan in some time. You think she struck out on her own?"

"Nah, she's alive. Juan Salazar fires his employees with a firing squad. Perhaps she's doing some side deals," the detective surmised.

"Who's the guy?" Brice wanted to know.

"That's for you to find out. They land in an hour!"

Toshiba rode along with the rookie to Atlanta's Hartsfield Airport. Their credentials got them in the secured part of the airport. Once the plane landed, they pulled their bag and searched it.

"Jack...fucking...pot!" an airport security agent announced when the search struck gold. Coke actually.

"Cocaine," Brice said shaking his head. A pair of Cameisha's cute little panties also caught his attention.

"We got a hit boss," Toshiba relayed into her phone to Walton back at the office.

"Let them pick it up and wait for my word. Nobody moves until I say," he ordered.

"You heard the man!" the airport cop said eagerly. The thirty-year-old black nerd loved making busts and was eager to make another.

****

"The fuck our shit at?" Trigga griped when he saw the same bag circulate the carousel twice. Cameisha knew in her gut that something was wrong. Every fiber of her being screamed 'Run!' but she wouldn't. She had too much invested and was too greedy.

'Get greedy, go to jail!'

"I know, I know, I know!" Meisha fussed at her father's memory causing Trigga to snap his head in her direction.

"Chill shawty, oh there it is!" he said when their bag magically appeared. Cameras rolled from several angles as he scooped it off the carousel.

Cameisha scanned every face that walked by. Anytime she made eye contact, she peered into their soul looking for a badge. Most people frowned at the odd girl and turned away. Not Agent Super-Cop though. He stared back, then ducked under a newspaper and stared some more. Meisha felt her heartbeat thundering in her throat when he got up and fell in step behind them.

"Aw man," she whined as she watched the bust unfold in slow motion. They were cooked and she knew it. Ten kilos in the bag was self-explanatory. Get greedy; go to jail.

"Fall back Agent Harst," Toshiba growled into her headset. The gung-ho cop was feet from the couple ready to take them down. If Detective Walton hadn't spoken up, he would have.

"Abort! Abort! Nobody move," he relayed urgently. "Brice, Toshiba, put a trail on them. Everyone, fall back."

"Sup with you shawty? You turning red!" Trigga informed Cameisha alerting her to the fact that she was holding her breath.

"Uh, nothing?" she said wondering why nothing happened. She surprised everyone when she hailed a taxi once they got outside.

"Sup shawty?" he wanted to know when she pushed him inside.

"Shit!" Toshiba fumed realizing they lost them. By the time they could reach their car, the taxi would be long gone.

Chapter 19

"You tripping' shawty!" Trigga declared dubiously when Cameisha relayed the events at the airport. "I ain't seen none of that! So why they ain't bag us?"

"I don't know!" she shouted a little harsher than intended. That had been eating at her the whole way home. Why let them go? Trigga not believing her only made it worse. She was sure of what she saw. They were caught and she knew it.

Cameisha stared out the window of the cab to be sure they weren't followed. She switched to the train and another taxi with Trigga complaining the whole way.

"Why don't you call them and ask them!" she murmured.

"Whatever! Tell you what though; once I finish this, I'm going back! With, or without you!" he shot back and turned his back to signal the end of the conversation. He got back to the task at hand which was cooking coke.

"Take a deep breath dickhead," Meisha mumbled under her breath seeing his surgical mask down around his neck. He pulled it up proving that he heard her.

Trigga hogged the stove cooking on two burners at the same time. He planned to cook one of his five kilos right then. Cameisha had to wait on the sideline until he finished. Once he did, he moved to the dining room table to weigh and bag while she moved to the kitchen.

"Un uh! Don't come in here," she chided Aqua when she waddled in. "You can't breathe this stuff!"

"Oops!" she said covering her mouth with her hand. She retreated back into the living room and shouted her request. "Can we go to that Halal place again?"

"Hell yeah!" Trigga answered for Cameisha. He dug in his pocket and came out with a hundred dollar bill. He was so grateful she found a replacement for the Fat-Fat burgers that he would gladly finance her new addiction.

"Sure we can," Meisha said as if Trigga hadn't even spoken. She was still in her feelings about the whole airport business. They were also going to look at a condo for her. "You ready to see your place?"

"Yeah, I guess," Aqua moaned sadly. She wasn't crazy about being alone now that Dasia was gone and Cameisha had a boyfriend.

"Don't worry mama, we getting a two bedroom 'cause I'll be spending plenty of nights over there," she said snarling at Trigga as she spoke. He made a 'yeah right' chuckle and kept on working without looking up.

"Well, bring some turkey burgers when you come," Aqua insisted.

Trigga finished separating the coke into eight 4.5-ounce packages. They would fix the G-packs once he got to Troy's apartment then supply the traps.

"See you later?" he asked as he stood to leave.

"Maybe," she quipped. It was a bold face lie though because she planned to be bent over the arm of that sofa that night.

"I know," he laughed patting the arm on his way out. It was a date!

****

"Come on in," Troy laughed sarcastically as Trigga used his key and walked in. Chaun tried to lift her head from his lap to speak but he held her in place. "Don't be nosy."

"Sup Chaun," Trigga said in passing. She waved since speech was out of the question with that much dick in her mouth.

Trigga laughed and settled down at the dining room table. He was still in eye and ear shot of the blowjob but didn't pay any attention to it. Instead, he got to work fixing up G-packs. The blowjob Chaun was giving was a lot less work than stuffing G-packs and they were up to almost 50 a day. At that rate, five kilos wouldn't last two weeks.

"I was worried about you cross that water shawty!" Troy called to him in the next room.

"Uh, can we wait till she done fo' we talk?" he laughed.

"That's what's...mmm...argh! Mm...shit!" Troy grunted and moaned as Chaun sipped the juice.

"Good! Now come help me bag this shit up," Trigga chided.

"I got you," he said getting his dick back from the girl. It was all shiny and clean from the blowjob as he put it away. He pulled a couple of twenties off a large roll of cash and handed it over.

"Thanks," Chaun smiled and leaned in for a kiss.

"Yeah, right," Troy laughed and walked away. "Lock the door behind you."

"Let me tell you 'bout this trip!" Trigga began and ended with the unseen drama at the airport.

"So you don't believe her? That ain't something no one would make up. She mighta just got paranoid with all that work," Troy reasoned. Trigga twisted his lips in careful consideration before speaking.

"I believe every word shawty ever spoke. Nah, she wouldn't make no shit up and that girl don't get paranoid!" he replied.

"So...what we gon' do?" Troy asked hopefully.

"I'on know shawty. Worse comes to worst, I may have to try it. If don't nothing else pop we ain't got no choice!"

Once they had enough work to resupply the traps they set out to make their rounds. They had to first collect the receivables from the night before, before restocking the shelves once more. Since they were already in Westfield that's where they started. The local dope boys passed close to ten grand into the car window and got broke off again. So far, so good, then it was off to Oak Tree.

"Hey Troy!" a flock of ghetto birds squawked as they drove through the complex. Troy just lifted a hand in a fake wave without even looking in their direction.

"Really? The whole crew huh?" Trigga laughed. He knew his friend well enough to equate his lack of interest to the fact that he ran through all of them. Troy was a conqueror. He was always on the hunt for new vaginas to vanquish.

"The whole crew!" he laughed and relayed which one had the best head, the best tail, etc.

"Err body out," Trigga nodded at the gathering of dope boys waiting on them. They would hate to have to go on a ghetto duck hunt. Those end just like a regular duck hunt, with a dead duck.

The trap stars broke bread, re-upped, and hit the trap. Everything was moving nice and smooth so they moved on to the next spot. When they reached Glen Valley, the dope boys gathered around.

"Even ol' Snake is...uh oh," Troy said then saw the dispirited look on his face.

"Uh oh is right, here comes the bullshit," Trigga said when he saw it. More proof came when he deliberately fell to the back of the line while everyone else jockeyed to be first.

One by one, the dealers forked over seven hundred and fifty dollars and got more work. They immediately rushed over to the trap where junkies were milling around waiting to be served. The young men puffed their chests out in pride when their count came correct. In return, they got more coke to sell. There were no pats on the back but they didn't get shot either. Besides, you can't spend accolades anyway. Just as expected, Snake's money was short.

"Only two...forty-three?" Troy winced painfully after counting it twice. Snake shifted from foot to foot like he was ready to bolt.

"Pay up nigga!" Trigga blurted happily. Snake flinched but he wasn't talking to him.

"You got that," Troy said and fished out his bankroll. Snake looked on in confusion as he counted out five hundred bucks and handed it over. He didn't know that the men had bet on just how short he would come. Troy figured it would be at least five hundred, but Trigga was nowhere near that optimistic.

"Ok, see what had happen was...ok first my mama, she be gambling, then, then I got robbed? Yeah robbed, some niggas in ski masks...the police ran up on me and I had to toss it and my mama," Snake rambled on a muddled collage of excuses.

"Un huh, oh! Damn!" Trigga and Troy nodded in bemused agreement. Even if any of it were true, it wouldn't have mattered. They gave their word that they would murder whoever came short. They intended to keep that promise and make another one just like it. He was short and was going to get shot. Nuff said.

"Ok, no problem. We done ran out of dope but shit, you wanna hit the club with us later?" Trigga offered.

"You for real? Hell yeah! Shoot I'm finna go shopping and get dead fresh!" he went on and on not realizing he had put himself in the air. Later that night, Trigga and Troy would simply kick away the chair.

Chapter 20

"Ok boy, I see you!" Cameisha cheered pulling up behind Bad Ass washing the new used car he'd just bought.

"Shit dope ain't it!" he said patting the Caddie like a puppy. "I'ma trick this shit out! Somebody too busy tricking to buy a car," he added pointing at Self on the porch getting cornrows.

"Say it ain't so?" she asked Self as he sat wincing from pain between Angel's thick thighs.

"No," Self said looking like he wanted to cry. He moved a little too much and got in trouble.

"Be still," Angel fussed and popped him with the comb. Bad Ass cracked up and Meisha just shook her head.

"I don't love them hoes," Bad Ass announced as he dropped the sponge in the bucket to follow her inside.

"And they're not going to love you either," she said over her shoulder. Self was grateful for the reprieve and got up to follow them inside.

Instead of following them into the kitchen, Self darted up the steps to collect the trap money. Eastwyck was doing 60 G-packs a day plus what Mama shuttled from the house. Self was sitting on over a hundred grand and glad to get rid of it.

Bad Ass and Self were splitting five to six thousand a day for running the show. Not bad for a couple of latch key kids from the Bronx. Self stacked most of his while Bad Ass balled. Clothes, shoes, jewels, and now a car. Self always shot Angel some mall money but it ain't tricking if it's your lady.

"Drop it in the bag," Meisha said when he shoved the cash under her nose. They were long past the counting money point. If it was anything other than what it was supposed to be, he would have told her. She was too busy double-checking the G-packs.

"A-yo, some niggas from over on Glenwood tryna cop some weight. I guess they pockets feeling a lil' light since err body coming for this butter," Bad Ass relayed.

"Stall 'em. We gotta nickel and dime this shit until I get a new connect," Cameisha replied as Angel stared on love struck by the female boss.

"Yo, go shopping," Self said passing off a stack of small bills that looked like a lot more than it was.

"Thank you!" Angel sang and took off to get Leera to go to the mall with her.

Once Cameisha gave them a whole key, she stood to leave. Both Self and Bad Ass walked her out and to her car. She and Bad Ass bumped fists but Self leaned in for an appreciative hug.

"I want a hug too!" Bad Ass whined. Meisha embraced him then shoved him away when he started grinding.

"Nasty ass lil' boy," she laughed and got in her car. No one moved until she was out of sight. Self went inside to cut and bag more G-packs to feed the demand, and Bad Ass took the work to the trap.

****

"Guess what?" Angel giggled as she and Leera entered the South DeKalb mall.

"Girl what?" Leera demanded hopefully. Hopefully it was something juicy or ratchet from her goody two shoes friend. She had been trying and failing to corrupt her for years.

"I think I'm pregnant! I mean, I'm pretty sure I am," she gushed and placed a hand on her hard, flat stomach.

"By who?" Leera stopped and asked. It would be a good question if she ever got pregnant, but it was just plain stupid to ask Angel.

"Yeah right! Girl you know I'm loyal to my man!" she snapped.

"Mph!" Leera huffed and turned her head like she had a secret she didn't want to tell. Angel didn't buy it for a second. If the girl had a secret, she would definitely tell it, embellish it, spread it, and broadcast it. Still, she bit and asked.

"Mph what?" Angel asked already twisting her lips into a 'yeah right' face.

"I'm just saying...you know I'm not one to gossip," she lied.

Angel cocked her head majestically, ready to defend her man. He was after all, the sponsor of the shopping excursion and many more that Leera benefitted from. The only thing she got out of Bad Ass was semen and even that got flushed. Meanwhile, Angel rocked the latest fashions and kept real cash in her knockoff purse.

"I'm just saying," she repeated as if that was saying something.

"You just saying what? If you got something to say then say it!" she said with the absolute last of her patience.

"Your man tried to fuck me. One night, I guess you were asleep, he came downstairs and put his dick in my face."

"And?" Angel asked knowing the story couldn't have ended there.

"And I told him I don't get down like that! You my girl, how I look fucking your boyfriend? Please! I don't even rock like that..."

"Oh, ok," Angel replied happily. She knew full well her friend was a snake. If Self put his dick in her face, she would have swallowed it whole like snakes do. She would have fucked it and whatever else could be done with a dick. Angel hadn't been with many dudes but Leera had gotten with all of them.

"You ain't mad?" Leera asked confused by the slow smile that spread on her face.

"Nope. Come on, let's go in here," she said dipping into the low budget lingerie store. Tameka's Rumors was the ghetto version of Victoria's Secret. Once inside, Angel picked out something for her man while Leera got something for mankind. It was a parting gift because Angel was officially done with her.

"Oh there go Boobie 'ndem from Glenwood," Leera exclaimed and rushed over to flirt with the dope boys. Angel walked outside and caught a taxi leaving them groping and feeling her up.

****

"Sup ma, you had fun?" Self called out from the kitchen when he heard Angel return. She didn't reply and marched upstairs to the bathroom. She had to pee and decided to kill two birds with one stone. Oh, and one rumor.

Self was sitting at the table cutting crack while Mama hovered near him waiting on him to finish it. She was so antsy she worked her hips as if she had an invisible hoola hoop while humming the theme music from "Different Strokes."

"It takes different strokes. It...oh hey babe," Self sang along until Angel walked in.

"You fucked Leera?" she demanded with a hand on her hip, tapping a foot. "Hey Mama."

"Huh? No! She sucked my dick though," he replied honestly and went on working.

"Wha...huh?" she frowned at the unexpected answer. "Why you ain't tell me!"

"I thought you told her to do it since you don't. It was that same night you said..."

"I know what I said!" Angel spat back. Oddly enough, she wasn't mad. How could she be mad when she told him to?

"Gotta suck a man's dick baby," Mama co-signed. "Me, I'll suck a..."

"Mama!" Angel grimaced holding up a hand to keep the uncomfortable comments from coming out of her mouth. The last thing any child wants to hear from a mother is about sucking dick. Mama shrugged and went back to hoola hooping and Angel turned back to Self.

"What is that?" he asked picking up the positive pregnancy test she tossed in the middle of his cocaine pile.

"That means you finna be a daddy," she said and squinted to watch his reaction.

"It does?" he asked examining the stick. Angel nodded her head and began to explain since the stick didn't speak.

"I'm pregnant," she said plainly then turned to her mother and repeated herself. "You finna be a grandma."

"Oh baby! That's gre...oh you finished!" she said but got distracted when Self finished bagging. "I need 12 for the fiddy."

"Here," Self said giving her the dope. She hopped in the air and clicked her heels and took off.

"Thanks Mama...sure, we can pick baby names," Angel said sarcastically to her mother's back.

"It is what it is," Self said to console her. His own mother ran out on him for the streets so he felt her pain. He had no idea if the woman was dead or alive. He never met his dad and wondered which one of the project men fathered him. "I'm happy about it!"

"You are?" Angel pleaded almost desperately. She never knew the comfort that only a daddy can bring. A lot of women waste a lifetime seeking to duplicate it or compensate for it. Some end up with men seeking to fill the void, but most end up with a lot of extra miles on their vagina while never finding it. Not Angel though, she had Self all to herself.

"Hell yeah I'm happy!" he cheered and scooped her in his arms. "Yo, you my girl. My wife, we getting married!"

"You asking me or telling me?" she demanded like it mattered. She would take it either way and she knew it. She would have to too because Self dropped to one knee, looked up, and said...

"I'm telling you!"

****

"That's fucked up yo' girl left you like that," Boobie said as he pulled in-to Eastwyck. He really didn't mind since it allowed him to fuck her in exchange for the ride home.

"Yeah that bitch feeling herself since her so-called man got the work," she huffed.

"Oh she fuck with shawty that be in the trap?" he schemed.

"No, the other one. He mainly stay in the apartment 'cause that's where they be keeping the work," Leera said with her trifling ass. She knew good and damn well, she just set a robbery in motion.

Chapter 21

"Ugh, the fuck?" Dasia grumbled when a sharp pain in her midsection snatched her from her slumber. Normally she and Lisa would sleep well into the afternoon after a night of snorting drugs and licking labia. The past few mornings she had been awoken by almost flu like symptoms.

"What's wrong bae?" Lisa asked hoarsely from just waking up herself.

"I'on know. I feel...horrible," she said mentally trying to track down where the ill feeling emanated from. It felt like her bones hurt.

"It's a bug going around. I hope we don't catch it," Lisa lied. Which was about anytime she opened her mouth. She had dealt with enough withdrawal symptoms to know what her friend was suffering from. Luckily, for both of them, she had the cure. "Let's get us a lil' wake up bump and eat something."

"Ok," Dasia agreed and watched her ass wiggle as she went to retrieve some dope.

Lisa had moved on from the speedballs and was snorting straight heroin. It was time for her girlfriend to get her next stripe as well. Dasia was no dummy and noticed the heroin wasn't coke. She had a quick decision to make as Lisa scooped some into a quill. As usual, she made the wrong decision and leaned in to snort some. Lisa move it away a little to make her pursue it. If she did, she would be pursuing it until the end of time.

Luckily, they had plenty of cash and plenty of drugs. Unluckily they were running through at an incredible clip. The ATM daily limit wasn't sufficient anymore. Not the way they shopped and partied like rock stars. Not the way the freeloaders freeloaded. Not the way Lisa skimmed and stole. Every time they set some coke or weed out, she set some to the side. Every time they hit the club, Dasia sponsored dope, smoke, and drinks.

"You like that boy huh? That diesel," Lisa cooed affectionately as Dasia swayed from the dope.

"Mmm, he's my boyfriend," she smiled as the warming glow of the heroin spread out through her soul. She leaned into a dope fiend lean while Lisa got ready to get her fix.

She pulled out her brand new works and got down to work. It had been a minute since she mainlined but it too was like riding a bike. After cooking up a small hit, she ran it up into a syringe through a piece of cotton as a filter. A vein volunteered as soon as she tied off her arm.

"Oh wow," Lisa exclaimed as the drug coursed through her being. A minute later, she was leaning too.

****

"Um...where the fuck is my Prada pantsuit?" Dasia demanded when a second search of both closets failed to produce it. "My Chanel shit, my Coogi! I'm missing mad shit I know I had!"

"Beats me, I can't find half my shit either," Lisa replied. They did so much shopping it was hard to keep track of what they bought. They didn't even keep track of what they spent or how much was left.

Neither girl could find some of their clothes because they were looking in the wrong place. Now had they searched Rita and Tina's closets they would have struck pay dirt.

"Fuck it, we some boss bitches! We'll just go shopping!" Lisa announced because again, it ain't tricking when it's somebody else's money. She pulled the tags off a designer sweat suit and stepped inside of it.

"That's right!" Dasia co-signed and did the same. "We got any cash?"

"Nah, we gotta stop by the bank," Lisa replied nonchalantly.

The first stop of the day was the local restaurant that fixed most of their meals. Sure, they spent thousands on pots and pans and gadgets for the kitchen, but no one used them. They always ordered a sampling of everything and ate a sample of all of it. It wasn't unusual for them to leave a hundred bucks poorer every time they went.

"Better get like ten bands. It's the weekend, you know we gotta turn up," Lisa advised when she pulled in front of the bank.

"Shit we better make it fifteen if we tryna turn up!" Dasia replied and hopped out. She knew Lisa's eyes were glued to her ass so she put a little something on her walk for her.

Dasia filled out a withdrawal slip for fifteen-thousand dollars and got in the long winding line. She felt the flurries of needing a hit while she waited. Lisa did too and took a few bumps in the car. She didn't dare try to shoot up in public, in broad daylight.

"I'm sorry, there are insufficient funds to cover this," the pretty teller advised apologetically when Dasia presented the slip.

"Huh? What you tryna say?" she shot back in confusion.

"Insufficient funds? Not enough money," she said winning the battle not to answer a silly question with a silly answer.

"I got...um? How much do I got?" Dasia frowned.

"Twelve thousand, four hundred, and eighty-two dollars. And thirty cents. Do you need a transaction statement?"

"I guess, anyway, give me twelve thousand then," she said and adjusted the withdrawal slip. She got the cash and rushed back to the car where Lisa had the dope waiting.

"We running out of cash," Dasia informed Lisa between snorts. "We may have to sell one of the kilos."

"Huh!" Lisa exclaimed stopping just short of asking what kilos. She had hit the cocaine so hard only a half a brick was left. "I know some niggas that will buy it. I'll have them meet us at the club."

"That's what's up. We finna turn up!" Dasia cheered and danced in her seat. Had she paid attention, she would have caught the side eye Lisa gave while she drove.

With the promise of selling a brick for 15 grand, the girls had no problem dropping five thousand at the mall. Dasia bought a thousand dollar Prada pantsuit for the second time. Shoes, blouse, and all the trimmings. Lisa would not be outdone and came up on a designer dress, heels, and purse.

Turn up!

****

Turn up is exactly what they did. First, they turned up in the VIP section of a trendy club. Then they turned up flutes of expensive champagne. Dasia turned up her nose at Tina when she turned up in the exact same Prada set. In her advanced state of inebriation, it didn't dawn on her that it was stolen from her closet. Nope, she was too busy worrying that they had the same clothes on.

Dasia, Lisa, Tina, Rita, and whoever else happened along took large hits out of a large baggie of cocaine that the girls brought along. Lisa's friend AJ walked in and scanned the room. They shared a conspiratorial nod and he made his way over.

"Sup Li-Li," AJ said as he and his partner in crime arrived. "This my man Chase."

"Sup AJ, this my girl...ok, then," Lisa said cutting short the introduction when she saw them making goo-goo eyes at each other. Chase was her complexion, six feet tall, and handsome. Just the kind of guy she liked when she liked guys. Lisa felt a stab of jealousy but shook it off. It could actually work in her plan. With her trifling ass.

"This my shit!" Dasia vowed when the DJ flawlessly mixed in Erv-G's latest banger. She tossed her hands in the air, closed her eyes, and danced in her chair.

"Come on," Chase said as he pulled her up by her hand. Dasia looked over to Lisa for approval or reaction.

"Go on girl, have fun. Turn up!" she said. Them dancing gave her and AJ a chance to solidify the plan. "You got that?"

"Shole do!" he said eagerly. He couldn't pass up a deal to trade two ounces of heroin for half a brick of coke.

Meanwhile, on the dance floor, Dasia was getting it in. She ran through a coke-fueled medley of the latest dances while Erv-G spit fire over a thunderous beat. When she spun around to put the booty on him, he grabbed her waist. Dasia felt her panties get wet and knees buckle as he grinded a rock hard erection against her ass. She had had enough. She grabbed him by the hand and pulled him back over to the table.

"I'm ready to go," she demanded. Dasia still gripped Chase's hand so there would be no misunderstanding of her intentions. She intended to fuck him, plain and simple.

"A one night stand means one night," Lisa clarified as she stood. The foursome left the club and went out to the parking lot. The boys got in their car and followed the girls to their condo. Once they arrived, Dasia led Chase to the guest room while Lisa and AJ plopped down on the sofa.

"Shit, you may as well let a nigga get a nut too," AJ reasoned since it was crystal clear what Dasia and Chase were going to do. He pressed the issue by leaning back and pulling his dick out.

"May as well huh?" Lisa said sarcastically and took it in her hand. It responded to her touch and grew hard as she watched. She spit on the swollen head, and then worked it in.

"Sss, go on, put that guy in ya mouth," he pleaded desperately.

"Un uh," she replied and stroked it. She put more saliva on it and used it as lubricant. The long, twisting strokes made his legs rock.

"Shit!" AJ grunted and sent a glob of semen high into the air. She kept on stroking as he erupted onto the coffee table. Kept right on pulling until his spasms came up empty.

"There, you got a nut," Lisa said and went to wash her hands. In the bedroom, Chase wasn't getting any resistance.

"Get...this...pussy!" Dasia demanded with each long, hard stroke of Chase's long, hard dick. She really didn't have to tell him to because he was doing just fine. She had been so starved for dick that she came every other thrust.

"Mm, mm, mm, hm!" Chase agreed. He snatched his bare dick out of her at the last second and used her juice to stroke himself and bust a nut all over her back.

"Whew, I needed that. You a beast with it," she complimented.

"Shit, you too! That pussy so good I hate to do this."

"Do what?" Dasia asked sitting up to talk. His reply came in the form of a hard right hook that knocked her out cold. He snatched the phone cord from the wall and quickly tied her up.

"You straight?" Chase asked as he came out of the room.

"Hell yeah, let's ride," AJ said since they'd already made the trade. He and Lisa traded nods of appreciation as he departed.

Lisa locked the door behind the robbers and rushed to open her package. She quickly fixed up a hit in her cooker. After plucking the barrel of the syringe to remove the deadly air bubbles, she eased it into a vein. She felt the effect of the good dope before the plunger reached the bottom.

"Mmm," Lisa moaned and laid back. She reached between her legs and quickly got herself off, then nodded with the needle still hanging out of her arm.

****

"Lisa! Lisa! Help me!" Dasia yelled when she awoke from the punch. The combination of the blow, other drugs, alcohol, lack of sleep, and turning up had kept her out until the next morning. That meant dope fiend morning sickness along with being tied up.

"Girl what you in here yelling about?" Lisa called out as she came down the hall. "Oh my God! What happened?"

"That dude, um...Chase, he tied me up. Punched me too!" she explained as she was untied.

"Girl they tied me up too!" Lisa lied. She did that a lot.

"So...how you get out? Why you ain't check on me?" she whined.

"Girl they robbed us! Took all the coke and all the money!" she replied ignoring the question. "All we got left is this."

"I need me a line," Dasia pleaded as she rubbed the marks left by the cord. Then reached up to touch the knot on her head. She noticed Lisa was unscathed but now wasn't the time to worry about it.

It was time to get high.

"Shoot we may have to shoot this lil' bit. This ain't gon' do shit for us if we try to snort it!" Lisa said referring to the two hit portion she separated from the rest. There was a quiet power shift, she was now firmly in charge.

"Um..." Dasia replied. That was good enough for Lisa so she whipped out the works. She watched curious as she cooked up the batch and filled the syringes.

"Let me see," Lisa instructed reaching for her arm. Dasia stuck it out like was about to get her blood pressure checked. She wasn't. Lisa tapped the fat vein that popped up. Curiosity killed the pin stick as the needle entered. Dasia twisted her lip inquisitively as she drew blood into the needle. Then slowly pushed her demise into her vein.

"I can feel it!" Dasia marveled as the effects could be felt before the plunger reached the bottom of the barrel. She leaned into a nod before Lisa ran her own dope. Soon, they were both nodding.

Dasia came around before Lisa did. Even high as a kite she felt lower than low. This was not what her new life was supposed to be. She suddenly missed her son, her mother, the Bronx, and her friends. The friends she had betrayed and stolen from. Suicide came to mind but was quickly shaken away. Instead, she grabbed her phone and called the only friend she had. The one true friend who was and would always be there. Whoever doesn't have one of those, it's because they aren't one themselves.

"Hey chica...eh em," she greeted clearing her throat.

"Dasia, is this...Dasia?" Aqua asked hopefully.

Chapter 22

Duck had been given the assignment of keeping an eye on Cameisha since he lived in Atlanta. He was in the courtroom with Suave when Bilal was sentenced. He followed her to her condo so they knew where she laid her head and with who. His surveillance over the last months uncovered some interesting information. It was time to call the boss.

"Boss! Boss! Guess what? You ain't gon' believe it! Take a guess! Boss!" Duck rambled.

"Get on with it!" Suave barked. He couldn't stand the man's theatrics in general but especially not first thing in the morning. The call had awakened him and his matching bed warmers Amber and Darla.

"My bad," Duck said apologetically like someone used to getting checked. "She's a dope girl! Got a whole complex on the eastside selling her work. Her boyfriend is a dope boy and he's spreading out on the westside. They fuck around and meet in the middle they gon' have the whole city on smash. 'Cept they ain't got no good connect. These Dominicans or whatever the fuck they are, are squeezing the city dry. They selling work out of the city for some reason. These local niggas gotta go outta town to cop. It's crazy! You get the pictures I sent?"

"Pictures?" Suave asked then paused to check his phone. Sure enough, there were several pictures messages waiting to be opened. He opened them and scowled at Cameisha. Twisted his lips at Cameisha and Trigga kissing and finally nodded at the shots of Cameisha's booty in a pair of tight jeans.

"No connect huh?" Suave repeated out loud even though he was talking to himself.

"What you want me to do Boss?" Duck asked faithfully.

"Nothing! Don't do shit...not until I get down there," he barked and hung up.

"You need anything daddy?" Amber asked with wide blue eyes.

"Head? Pussy? Sandwich?" Darla added just as eager to please.

133

"I'll take some head and a sandwich," he said pulling the blanket away to reveal his morning hard on. The girls clinked heads like a toast as they both dipped low to get the dick. Amber was a little swifter and claimed her prize.

"Aw man!" Darla whined and got out of the bed. She stomped off childishly to go make the sandwich.

Suave grabbed the back of Amber's blonde head and slammed it up and down on his dick. He literally jacked off using her face. He had far more dick than she had throat and gagged her with every stroke.

"Grr!" he growled as he erupted in her mouth. She was forced to swallow in big gulps or drown. Darla watched jealously from the door. Once the spasms ended, she came and presented the sandwich complete with turkey, cheese, lettuce, tomatoes, and a subservient bow.

"Get my phone!" he ordered and bit into the sandwich. "Get Mo on the line!"

****

"Sup Boss, who the girl?" Mo asked of the pictures that came just before the call. He asked about the girl even though he liked the guy. With his gay ass.

"Never mind her, what's up with my punk ass, bitch ass, goody two shoes ass, captain save these hoes ass, um…good Samaritan ass, bitch ass brother?" Suave wanted to know. He let out a long yawn from the effects of the white girl head and sandwich.

"Same shit boss. That nigga won't fuck with us. Won't eat with us, smoke, nothing," Mo reported.

"What about ol' Lucy, she get anywhere with him?" Suave asked about the female officer they had on payroll. She snuck in the contraband and provided much needed sexual favors. Nothing breaks up the monotony of prison life like a shot of pussy. Real pussy, not the boy pussy Mo was fond of.

"Got cursed out! He wouldn't even let her blow him! Said he's just gonna do his time and move on with his life," Mo relayed.

"Shit! He ain't got much time. It may be time to turn up the heat."

"How high?" Mo asked hopefully. He'd raped dudes on Suave's orders before and would gladly do it again.

"That's up to him. Take him the phone. If he don't get with my program then put him on your program. Not too deep though, he is my brother after all!" Suave cracked up maniacally.

Mo stuck the phone in his pocked and rushed over to Bilal's cell. He barged in without knocking as a show of disrespect.

"Come on in why don't you?" Bilal hissed sarcastically like a teenage girl. It made Mo so hard, so quickly, he almost forgot what he was there for.

"Oh!" he snapped remembering the phone. He pulled it out and put it on speakerphone. "Here he is Boss."

"What's up you bitch ass, punk ass nigga? You ready to straighten your face and kill that bitch who put you in there?"

"Stop calling her a bitch!" Bilal yelled at the top of his lungs. It was so bitchy it turned Mo on even more. "I told you I have forgiven her. I love her. I'm going to marry her so you may as..."

"Show him the pictures," Suave cut in, cutting off the sucker for love soliloquy.

"Like this?" Mo asked showing a picture of Meisha and Trigga.

"So! That could be her brother for all you know!" Bilal insisted.

"Oh?" Mo laughed and swiped to the next picture. The one with the couple French kissing and they aren't French. "And this? And this..."

"I won't do it! I won't hurt her no matter what," he said firmly.

"Final answer?" Suave dared.

"Final answer!" he insisted crossing his arms and turning his head. Just like a woman scorned.

"Rape him!" Suave ordered and hung up. He was a sociopathic piece of shit but even he didn't want to hear a man get raped.

The first time Mo raped Bilal he was mad at Mo. He didn't have to be so rough. The next rape, the next day he was mad at his brother. The next day he was mad at his mother for birthing him. The day after that he was mad at himself. It took a week before his anger shifted in the right direction...

Mo was deep in his anus when it dawned on him that it was indeed Cameisha's fault. She used him to order the pills, and then turned her back on him. He lost his medical license, condo, respect, freedom, and anal virginity. He was finally mad enough to kill. He let Mo finish and told him, "Call my brother, I'll kill her."

Chapter 23

I bear witness that there is no God but I. I'm the reason why...

"You're a fuckin' dumb ass is what you are!" Jackie shouted at the radio. She literally slammed the buttons to stop the assault on her soul. The blasphemy affected her so badly she didn't just turn the station; she turned it off completely. She turned on the TV to try to wipe the bad taste from her psyche but dumb ass was there too.

"Yeah dis your boy Verb; here promoting my fuck school campaign. I ain't never learnt shit in no school and look how rich I is!" he explained in a TV interview.

She could only shake her head as she watched. The man was actually handsome before he started getting tattoos on his face. Random phrases and curse words adorned his face like graffiti. The popular rapper had a cult like following hanging on his every word. Doing whatever his dumb ass said do. Last week it was drink till you throw up, this week, fuck school.

Verb was born Vernon Russell in a small town in Alabama. He didn't farm like the rest of the townsmen because he was too dumb. Technically, his low IQ put him in the mental retardation category. He qualified to get a check.

Except he was handsome, cool, and funny enough to earn a following. You see, somewhere along the line, black people got life fucked up. As long as they could be a part of something, they were happy. As long as they could shout their clique, posse, or gang they were cool. In the generations past, that was called dick riding, and dick riding is not cool at all.

Verb was so influential as a youth that his peers all started doing poorly in school to impress him. Dumb was suddenly cool and the special education class was the place to be. The school had to swap the short bus for a long one to accommodate them.

Rap music had dumbed down enough for his nursery rhymes to catch on. He became a local celebrity then went viral. The next thing you knew he moved to the ATL and blew the fuck up. Jackie felt her own IQ plummet as she watched the interview.

"I'm bigger than Martin Luther the King! What he ever do? He ain't go double platinum! He ain't have his own dance! And tell me who da fuck name dem self after a skreet?"

By the time, he said he was God, Jackie couldn't take it anymore. She covered her mouth and retched from the stupidity. She pulled the plug from the wall and wrapped it up.

"Hey babe you wanna go...what are you doing?" Ralphie wondered when he walked in on her lifting the TV to the open window ready toss it out.

"I don't want it anymore," she vowed. "He made me dumb!"

****

"You go boy!" Cameisha looked down and cheered. Trigga smiled and kept on sliding his tongue in and out of her. He switched to circling her swollen love button and pushed her right to the edge. "I'm going to cu..." The satellite phone rang pausing time.

Cameisha sprang out of the bed and snatched the phone off its cradle. Her heart stopped thinking it could be her daddy. Poor Trigga looked so confused with his wet face. The letters U.K on the caller ID flipped her frown into a smile.

"Uncle Killa!" she cheered trying to catch her breath.

"Sup Meisha, you ok? Your voice is trembling," he replied.

"Huh? Yeah I was just...Hey Uncle Killa!" she replied at a loss for words. She might have been a dope girl and a dangerous girl but she was still, a girl.

"Oh, ok, um sorry to interrupt," Killa said catching on. "I need your help."

"Shit, anytime, anyplace!" she shot back. She didn't ask what or why because it didn't matter. When it came to her family, anybody could get it. Anywhere, anytime.

"A'ight, meet at the zoo in an hour," he replied.

"The Atlanta Zoo? You're in the A?" she shouted happily.

"Nah, Paris Zoo. One hour," Killa snapped sarcastically and hung up.

"I know you gonna explain something," Trigga announced when she put the phone down. All he knew was it was the family line and not to touch it. He couldn't even have the number.

"When I get back bae. We only got ten minutes!" she urged.

They had to make the most of those ten minutes so they ran into the living room. Cameisha fell over the arm of the sofa and Trigga plunged inside of her. He went to work with long, hard strokes that echoed in the room. He picked up his pace when she began to shiver and shake beneath him. She could be a selfish lover at times and conk out once she got off.

Cameisha squealed out when she came then contracted her muscles to get him off. It did the trick and he collapsed on her back. He wouldn't get to catch his breath though.

"Get up! I gotta go," she said pushing up. She bolted back into the room and got dressed to kill. Not cocktail dress and heels dressed to kill, but black jeans, black sneakers, and a black gat. Dressed to murder.

"What you got going on?" he asked seeing the gun.

"Family business, babe. Love you," and a kiss was all he got out of her. She used her regular phone to call Jackie on the way out.

"Yo, get dressed. I'm on my way!"

****

"Ain't the zoo closed?" Jackie asked as they pulled into the darkened parking lot. On cue, a flashlight flashed on and off.

"There he go," Cameisha said and took off in that direction. As they neared a gate opened and a man in a zoo uniform waved them in. Meisha wasn't afraid in the least because she knew God was with her. That and a gun.

"Thanks Mr...Wali," she said reading his name off his tag. It was he who was grateful as he watched both girls' asses shift in the moonlight.

"My pleasure," he told both sets of cheeks with a tip of his hat. "Over by the lion's den!"

That's exactly where she found her uncle. He and the male lion sat staring at each other. Two killers bonding and along came two more.

"Hey Unc!" Cameisha screamed and ran into his embrace. The Lion King turned and walked away shaking his head.

"Sup niece," he grunted from almost having the wind knocked out of him. During the hug, he looked Jackie up and down with one of those 'Damn she fine!' frowns on his handsome face. "Who's your friend?"

"Oh, this my girl Jackie. Killa meet Jack, Jack meet Killa. My uncle!" she stressed when she started batting her eyes at him.

"Hello Jackie. You got a man?" he asked as they shook hands. Killa peered so deeply into her eyes she forgot about ol' Ralphie at home.

"No," Jackie giggled and ducked her head shyly.

"Un huh! Yes you do!" Cameisha snitched.

"Oh yeah! I almost forgot about him," Jackie laughed and snapped out of her trance. She kept that hand though.

"Nice to meet you. If my niece trusts you I know you can be trusted," Killa said getting a smile out of Cameisha. It was a safe bet though because snakes hang with snakes.

"So who gotta go bye-bye?" Meisha asked. She was ready to knock off whoever so she could get back in her bed with her man.

"Y'all ever heard of this rapper who calls himself Verb?" he asked. Jackie immediately retched at the mention of his name.

"I hate that dude! He got kids dropping out of school, using drugs, reckless sex..." Jackie went on and on.

"That clown with the writing on his face? Words misspelled, talking 'bout he's God! Please let me murk that nigga Unc!" Cameisha pleaded placing her palms together as if in prayer. The male lion seemed to pick up on the violence and let out a low growl in approval. She looked at the big cat, her uncle, and put it all together. A slow smile spread across her face and she said, "Or you handle it."

"I need you to lure him to me. I'll handle it from there."

"No problem Unc. Oh! I have a...situation. I need guns, bombs, and a tank if you can get it.

"Holla at my man Big Shawn. Tell him I sent you," Killa replied retrieving the number from his phone.

"You want me to stay with him while you go get the Verb guy?" Jackie offered.

"Girl no! Besides, you can help me lure the nigga to his death."

****

A few nights later Cameisha and Jackie went to see Verb live in concert. They were both pretty sexy in mid-thigh dresses showing plenty of leg and plenty of tittie. They just knew they were sexy enough to catch his attention. They weren't even close.

"The fuck!" Jackie grimaced when they waded into the crowd. The teen and young women were damn near naked.

"Look at this bitch!" Meisha said when a topless teen walked by. They got nowhere close to their target looking like church ladies. Jackie had to rush into the bathroom to throw up halfway through the first song. They accepted defeat and retreated to try again. If you can't beat 'em, join 'em.

Verb had a show in a downtown club and Cameisha and Jackie were in the place. Both had to change into their THOT costumes after they left the house because both had men who would not let them out of the house like that.

Daisy Dukes left half of their ass cheeks hanging from the bottom. Half shirts made of sheer material completely showed their breasts. They felt like fools, but it did the trick.

"Hol' up! Who y'all bitches?" Verb had to know when they traipsed past him in the VIP. Both girls acted like they hadn't seen him. Cameisha actually flinched at being called a bitch to her face. Luckily, Jackie grabbed her arm to prevent her from punching him in his foul mouth.

"I'm Jackie and my gi...um bitch Cameisha," Jackie said trying not to laugh.

"Jack! Why you using our real names?" Meisha asked through clenched teeth like a ventriloquist.

"This dude is a house plant! Besides, ain't like he gon' live to tell anyone," Jackie reasoned. Dude was an inanimate object and didn't understand his murder being discussed right in front of him. He had a one-track mind and spoke what was on it.

"I wanna fuck both y'all bitches. At da same damn time," he announced. 'I Wanna Fuck' was the name of one of his songs. It worked great as a pick up line in the past and worked that time too.

"Okay," Cameisha and Jackie sang in unison like bookend groupies.

"Let's ride den!" Verb cheered. On cue, his bodyguards stood to guard his body. Cameisha twisted her lips ruefully, hoping they had life insurance.

"They don't gotta come," Jackie said in an effort to spare them.

"Dey gotta go err where I go. My record label said so. Dey not gonna see us fuck dough. Unless you want them to?" Verb replied.

"We can go to my place. That way y'all ain't got to drop us off after you fuck us," Meisha explained.

"Sounds like a good idea boss," one of the bodyguards said while the other co-signed by nodding his head. They were the ones who had to do the drop offs so they were eager to save a trip. A mistake they would not live to learn from.

"It would be safer than taking them to your residence," the other guard added.

"Ok," Verb shrugged. He had no idea what the word residence meant and didn't want to ask in front of the girls. Wouldn't want to look dumb you know.

****

"Here?" the driver asked when he pulled to a stop in front of a darkened building.

"Yup," Meisha said and got out. The guards got out first to make sure it was safe. It wasn't.

As soon as they stepped on the sidewalk, they both dropped dead. Verb looked down at them in his everyday confusion trying to figure out what just happened. He figured it out when Killa stepped from the shadows. The billowing from the tip of the silencer-equipped pistol said all that needed to be said. Verb assumed it was a robbery and lifted his chin, ready to accept it.

"Ugh!" Killa grunted and socked Verb with everything he had. The blow broke his jaw on both sides and put him to sleep. He wouldn't be saying anymore dumb shit that night, ever for that matter.

"About my beef. How can I get to a nigga I can't catch out in the open?" Meisha asked as Killa drug Verb into the backseat.

"A funeral. Kill someone he loves and catch him at the funeral," he suggested. With his violent ass.

"Good idea." She smiled and nodded knowing exactly who she was going to kill. Her uncle tossed a set of keys once he had Verb in the car.

"That blue one," he said pointing to a sedan down on the corner. She and Jackie rushed over but found the key didn't work. They turned around just in time to see Killa pull off.

"Hey!" Cameisha wailed knowing she was about to miss the main event. She pressed a button on the remote and another car on the next block honked and flashed its lights.

"Guess I better change. Trigga would lose his damn mind if he saw me come in like this," Meisha sighed.

"That's exactly why I'm keeping mine on!" Jackie said wickedly.

****

Verb got the best sleep he'd had in months. He snored loudly from the punch, the drugs, alcohol, and constant turning up. Killa called his name several times when they reached their destination but he didn't budge.

"Rise and...something," Killa said pouring his soda on him. "Get up and get out!"

Verb woke up and tried to say some dumb shit but his broken jaw wouldn't allow it. It came out like the alphabet, which was odd because Verb didn't know the alphabet.

Killa walked him by gunpoint into the deserted zoo. Once they were in, he fired a silent shot into his ass cheek. He hopped, shimmied, and shook like his latest dance.

"Lmnop?" he asked wondering what was going on.

"I'm going to count to ten, and then I'm coming after you. If I catch you, I'm going to kill you," he explained quite eloquently.

Verb knew how to count to ten and took off when Killa reached two. He had never been to the zoo before and had no idea where he was going. He ran zigzagging, darting his eyes in every direction.

"Quick, in here! He won't follow you in there," Wali said holding a door open for him. Verb nodded his thanks and ducked inside. Wali closed and locked the door then went around front with Killa to watch the show. When he hit the lights, it was show time.

The lions were sniffing the fresh blood in the air when the lights came on. The man-eaters couldn't believe they actually had a man to eat. Verb couldn't believe his eyes either. He blinked and rubbed them but the lions were still there.

Female lions generally do the killing but when they eased forward, the king let out a roar that called them off. This one was his.

"Hijk!" Verb shouted and took off running. He ran around the lion den as the lion stalked him.

"Tell them you're God and you created them!" Killa yelled and cracked up.

"No, no, turn up! Turn up!" Wali laughed getting in on the fun.

Verb ran out of room and the lion pounced. He tried to fight and threw a punch but the lion ate it. Literally, he snatched his whole arm off. He clamped down on his neck and nearly severed his head. Once the man stopped kicking, the girls moved in and shared the meal.

"I wouldn't post that," Wali advised seeing Killa capture the kill on his phone.

"Nah, for my personal viewing pleasure," he lied. He knew good and well he was going to post that video.

Turn up!

Chapter 24

"Boy I got us a lick!" Boobie announced to his right hand man called Suspect. He had the right name too because in his scant 22 years on the planet he had been a robbery suspect, a rape suspect, and a murder suspect. He was the very definition of a suspect ass nigga.

Boobie and Suspect belonged to a notorious robbing crew. They had hit jewelry stores, convenience stores, check-cashing places, and even a bank. Their favorite meal however was dope boys. Dope boys usually had no surveillance, no security, and damn sure couldn't call the police. And say what? 'Niggas stole my dope?'

"You already know I'm down," Suspect replied. He didn't ask who or what because it didn't matter. Anybody could get it as far as he was concerned. He had a reputation of an itchy trigger finger, known not to leave any witnesses. Dead people do not make good witnesses. Who's going to believe them?

"Them New York ass niggas done set up shop in Eastwyck. Got that good ass dope but won't sell no weight. Little nigga offered to let me work a pack but fuck that. That lil' hoe Leera put me up on the stash spot!"

Suspect watched his friend pace back and forth. His odd gait always amused him. Boobie was so slew footed it looked like he had his shoes on the wrong feet. Then, on top of that, he thought it cool to dip to each side with every step. He looked sort of like a clock pendulum from a distance. He just knew he had a mean swagger but really looked like a fool. Because a fool and his money soon part, he was always able to keep a hoe on deck. A hoe in the hand beats...nothing actually.

The dastardly duo decided not to include the rest of the crew on the lick. They weren't sure just how much they were working with and thought 50/50 would be best. What Boobie didn't know is that, if the haul was enough, Suspect would have left him there with the other dead bodies and split the money with himself.

****

"Yeah something going on, fo' sho'," Boobie said nodding in agreement with himself. They set up surveillance on the house to see what they could see. Mama shuffled in and out while Bad Ass came and went several times to drop off money and pick up dope.

"Told you so," Leera said interrupting the blowjob. She held his dick in hand speaking into it like a microphone, while Suspect played under her dress from the backseat.

"How we gon' play it? Wild cowboy?" he suggested since that was his preference. Left up to him he would run in and murder everything moving then go through their pockets.

"Nah, we gotta be smart," Boobie replied. He pointed at Leera's bobbing head to remind him she was a witness. Suspect shrugged like 'So?' since he had no problem killing her too. "Member last time..."

"True dat," Suspect said twisting his lips. The last time they pulled a wild cowboy style lick they left a hundred grand behind with the dead man. That man most certainly would have parted with it to stay alive. That was a real lose-lose situation.

"I can get y'all in. Just break me off a lil' dough," Leera suggested.

"Do it!" Boobie demanded before offering her a drink. As soon as she swallowed, she hopped in the backseat to take care of Suspect.

****

"Hey baby, I ain't seen you in a minute," Mama greeted when she let Leera in on her way out. "Angel! You got company!"

"I do?" Angel asked Self, who of course couldn't answer. She twisted her lips at his helpless shrug and got out of the bed. She pulled his shirt over her shorts and went to investigate. Angel only had one friend who she had cut off weeks earlier, so imagine her surprise to see Leera standing in the living room.

"Hey girl! Who's here?" Leera asked darting her eyes around.

Her presence was odd enough to make Angel overlook her odd de-meanor. Leera smiled fraudulently despite the look of disgust on her once friend's face.

"What are you doing here?" Angel asked with a pained expression.

"Girl stop! We ain't finna let no nigga come between us are we?" she asked as if the notion was ludicrous.

"Eh, yeah!" Angel replied because it wasn't.

"Girl we bigger than that! I brought us a blunt of that loud so we can kiss and make up. 'Cept I ain't kissing you 'cause I don't know where yo' lips been," Leera giggled.

"I know where your lips been though!" How you gonna..." Angel shot back but was cut off by Self descending the stairs. "I'm pregnant. I ain't finna smoke no weed!"

"Oh, ok," Leera said hanging her head in dejection. The show of contrition worked and Angel opened her big heart once again so the snake could slither in.

"Sup?" Self asked when he arrived. He heard about the blunt and forgave her already. Not exactly magnanimous since he got his dick sucked after all.

"Nuffin," Angel said mocking his accent. "Leera came to smoke a blunt with you."

"And watch a movie!" Leera cheered holding up the "Yung Pimpin'" DVD.

"I'll sit between y'all so his dick don't end up in nobody's mouth," Angel said dryly. She got her little shot off but took the chair across the room to avoid the smoke.

Self lit the blunt and almost choked when the hilarious movie be-gan to play. Angel giggled but was more interested in Leera's antics. She shot a glance at Self, her, the door, and back to Self. She had just opened her mouth to ask what was up when the door eased open and answered for her. Self sat up when the two masked men walked in behind their guns.

"Y'all be easy," Suspect said from behind a ski mask. He could afford to be cordial since he had an AK-47.

"We just here fo' the money and the dope," Boobie explained. Angel recognized him instantly from his voice and duck walk, but knew enough to keep quiet.

"Shit if you know we got that you must know where it is," Self said shooting Leera a side eyed scowl and hit the blunt.

"As a matter of fact, I do," Boobie said. He tucked his pistol and hit the steps. Self extended the blunt to Suspect while they waited.

"May as well," he shrugged and plucked it from his fingers. He took two puffs and passed it back according to protocol. The charitable act saved three lives because Suspect had just decided to chill. "And it's that loud!"

"Keep it," Self offered. He could only shake his head at how easily he got robbed. He counted up over 30 grand and several ounces of crack. It should be enough to keep them alive. A lot of robberies turn into murders when the haul isn't sufficient. If the stick up men think you're holding out, they'll kill you. Reason being if they can't have it, you can't either. His mind went to his new pistol under the pillow and hoped it wasn't found.

It was the one he planned to use on the get back. He had bust his gun plenty of times back in the Bronx, but didn't have any bodies on his soul. Not yet anyway.

"We straight!" Boobie announced happily as he came bounding down the stairs. His demeanor indicated he had struck big.

"Straight-straight?" Suspect checked.

"Straighter than straight!" he assured him moving towards the door.

"A'ight, y'all be easy," Suspect nodded as he departed. All three let out sighs of relief when they heard tires squealing from the hasty retreat.

"Shit you may as well have went with them," Self told Leera.

"Me? Huh? Wha..."

"What my ass! You did this! Remember, I know you!" Angel snapped. She knew her friend had set up at least one robbery.

"Y'all tripping! I ain't finna stay here and be insulted!" she huffed and stormed out.

"What we gon' do?" Angel asked with tears streaming down her face. She felt partly to blame by letting her friend know too much of her business. A common mistake made by many women. Bragging about how well your man in laying the pipe but shocked when your friends fuck him behind your back. It's your fault for advertising his dick slinging skills.

"Bout to call my sister!"

Chapter 25

"Turkey burger express! Did someone order 50 turkey burgers?" Cameisha called out playfully as she used her key to enter Aqua's condo. Aqua was yapping away on her phone but quickly hung up when she walked in.

"That wasn't Dasia!" Aqua blurted and tossed her phone aside.

"Um...o...kay?" Meisha laughed in amusement. She took a couple of burgers and fries from the bag and went to put the rest in the fridge.

Cameisha admired the cute two bedroom she'd copped for her friend. It was located in downtown Decatur near the courthouse. A few miles away from Eastwyck though worlds apart. Aqua had already destroyed one of the burgers by the time she returned.

"I can't wait to have this baby! I'm tired of peeing every five minutes!" She grumbled and hoisted herself up.

"And I can't wait to meet my niece or nephew!" Cameisha called behind her as she waddled to the bathroom. She glanced at Aqua's phone and recalled her odd statement. Curiosity got the best of her so she picked it up and checked the call log. She could only shake her head at the contact labeled 'Not Dasia.'

"I'm coming to see you real soon," Cameisha texted with an evil grin. She jotted down the number for later use. As soon as time permitted, she was going to kill her. The phone buzzed from Dasia's reply.

"Can't wait."

"Whew!" Aqua said as she waddled back down the hall. Meisha put the phone back and took a bite of her burger.

"I...hold on," Meisha said and paused to check her own vibrating phone. She hit the ignore button when she saw it was Self since he was her next stop. He called right back indicating it was important since everyone knew how much she hated someone blowing her phone up. The spoiled brat refused to even check her voicemails. "Sup yo?"

"We got hit," Self blurted out animatedly.

151

"Police?" Cameisha asked terrified. Her eyes were as wide as dinner plates.

"Nah, stick up kids. Niggas ran up in here with choppers. My girl knows who it was. That bitch Leera set that shit up," he said in one breath.

"Slow down B. What they take? Y'all ain't hurt are you?" she asked noticing she asked about the money before their safety. The thought made her shake her head. Self was more important than money.

"Yo, they got all the work, about thirty in cash. I had a few racks in my pants they ain't get plus my personal stash," he said proving just how loyal he was without even trying. If he had any serpent in his system, he would have written those extra thousands into the robbery and kept them.

"I'm on my way!" she growled and hung up. She scrolled through her contacts looking for Big Shawn's number. She needed more guns. She planned to make an example of them.

****

"What happened?" Cameisha demanded as soon as Self opened the door to let her in.

"Like I said, we were..."

"Not you, her!" Meisha said turning to Angel. Angel's eyes grew wide just from the violent timbre of her voice.

"It was my friend, well, used to be friend Leera. She did this. She put Boobie and dem on the lick. She did it once before that I know of."

"The 'and dem' is more than one person?" she asked seeking clarity. People in the south will refer to one person as 'and dem' at times. Like my mama and dem when it's just their mama.

"It was two people. They had on masks but I know Boobie from that crazy walk. I know they stay over on Glenwood too," she explained. As she spoke Bad Ass tapped twice and came in. Even though he announced his presence, he had guns pointed at his face.

"Chill," Bad Ass uttered and Cameisha and Self lowered their weapons. "Yo, I just beat my feet with Capo, I know where they at right now. Gimme the word and we'll take care of them."

"Who is the other nigga?" Self asked.

"Some nigga called Suspect. We need to move now so we can get our shit back!"

"Nah, chill. Let 'em keep that lil' shit. They earned it. We 'bout to turn that Suspect into a victim!" Meisha proclaimed.

****

"Just tell me who and where and me and Troy will go handle that shit!" Trigga vowed as he drove towards Norcross.

"Troy and I," Cameisha corrected and instantly regretted it.

"You and Troy? Nah, me and Troy! Do them just like we did that lil' nigga Snake," he shot back.

Trigga and Troy definitely made a statement when they made an example out of Snake. A few more trappers were set to short the dope boys when they saw he got away with it. Not only did they not say anything, but invited him out on the town. Snake's dumb ass went shopping with the stolen loot. He was dead fresh when Trigga and Troy arrived but just plain dead by the time they left.

Trigga blew a hole in him with the shotgun that was so big you could see clear through. He did it right out in the parking lot in front of everybody. Their collection was hundreds of dollars over that night. Troy told them better not nare nigga call the police, and no one did. Snake laid in that parking lot for two days before he got scooped up. Police just happened by and saw him minus his new tennis shoes. He had gotten rained on and everything.

"Ok, first..." Cameisha began then decided to forego the grammar lesson. "Anyway, this is my beef and I gotta handle it. My people gotta do this; Self gotta get his hands dirty. He got violated and he gotta straighten it."

The mood was already tense since they both just cooked the last of their dope. They both whipped an extra quarter key out of it to stretch it. With that, they lost their edge. Now they had the same dope as the competition. They needed a new connect quick, fast, and in a hurry. If not Trigga planned on trying his luck with Belize.

"Besides, my uncle said to get at this dude for guns," she added, restarting the conversation.

"So when I'm 'posed to meet this so-called uncle of yours?" Trigga asked and got ignored. Cameisha turned her attention to the cars on the highway as if she hadn't heard the question or its implications. Sometimes the best way to end an argument is not to participate. Hard to argue with yourself.

"Exit here," she said repeating the GPS directions. A few turns later, they reached Big Shawn's apartment complex.

"Dude 'posed to have all this heat but stay in some 'partments?" Trigga chided and got ignored some more. She dug in her purse and pulled out her satellite phone and a maxi pad. She tossed the pad on his lap and dialed her uncle.

"Oh, oh, so I'm on my period huh? Sho nuff," Trigga said following her to the apartment.

"Hey Unc, I'm here," she said when Killa took the call. They walked up a flight and she knocked on the door. Waited, and then knocked again, then once more. It took several minutes before Big Shawn accepted that whoever the unannounced visitor was they weren't leaving.

"Yes?" Shawn asked behind a deceptive smile. Behind him was a .50 caliber Desert Eagle that wasn't so friendly.

"Um...hey!" Cameisha smiled and waved. "I'm Cameisha, my uncle, Killa. He um...here?"

Big Shawn frowned at the satellite phone for several seconds before taking it. He shot daggers back and forth between the two and put it to his ear.

"Yeah...uh huh...I bet...boy I swear!" he said as Killa made nice on the other end. In the end, he handed the phone back and turned around. "Come on."

"Yes!" Cameisha quietly cheered realizing they were in.

"Bet this nigga ain't got shit we couldn't get at the pawn shop," Trigga grumbled. Their host heard him and chuckled as he led the way to the showroom.

"In here," Big Shawn said opening the door and stepping aside.

"Told you this was some bulls...oh my!" Trigga swooned. He grabbed a table when his knees buckled upon entering. The walls as well as tables were loaded with all kind of guns and killing apparatus.

"You ok baby?" Cameisha asked catching him from behind. He couldn't see the 'I told you so' grin pasted on her fact. It didn't last long though.

"Damn! I...I...Damn!" she repeated when she got a gander at all the hardware in the room.

"Bae, my dick got hard. Look," Trigga said sheepishly and pointed at the lump in his jeans.

"If I had a dick it would be hard too," she assured him.

"Sounds like someone I know," Shawn laughed. He then slipped on his salesman hat and got down to business. "War or beef?"

"A lil' of both," Meisha replied. With all the other stuff going on, she almost forgot about Juan. He killed her friend and tried to kill her. She planned to evict him off the planet the first chance she got. A crate of grenades caught her eye so she went to investigate. "How much for these?"

"Five hundred each, but I'll throw one in for every ten grand you spend."

"I gots to have this!" Trigga proclaimed holding up a Calico sub-machine gun.

"What about this?" Meisha threw in holding an MP-5. They tag teamed poor Bigs asking about item after item. The mood was jovial, festive even until they saw it.

"What in *thee* fuck is that?" Trigga asked pointing at a mannequin in the corner. The other two mannequins in the room showed off bulletproof vests. The one he pointed at had on a suicide vest loaded with explosives.

"That is Sampson. Like from the bible. That's that shit you use when you gotta kill somebody so bad that you don't mind going with them," Bigs explained.

Cameisha got in her feelings knowing it was what her beloved grandfather had used. He'd stepped in for his son and killed his adversaries along with himself. She snarled at Bigs now realizing where he got it from. She quietly walked over and fondled it. She picked up the detonator and stopped just short of pressing the red button. Bigs knew it wasn't armed, but still frowned.

"How much for something like this?" she wondered without turning around.

"It's not for sale! Besides, this works a lot better," he said showing off a long-range sniper rifle with large silencer.

"I'll take it," she agreed. At the end of the shopping trip, they had two .22s, four .44s, nine .9mms, two Mac-10s, and a .40 caliber. Several bulletproof vests, the sniper rifle, and a grenade, finished their order. The total was over ten grand so he threw in an extra grenade. They loaded up the guns, a shitload of ammo, and went on their way.

"Bae, can we stop by the mall so I can pick up something to wear on my date?" Meisha asked referring to her upcoming rendezvous with Boobie and them.

"Now? With grenades in the trunk? Girl stop!"

****

"Who the fuck is that bitch?" Boobie exclaimed loud enough to offend the object of his desire.

"I ain't never seen that hoe," Suspect said proving why he had earned all those Ds in school.

Cameisha turned, turned her nose up at them, and then turned back to the counter. She had been in and out of that corner store all day waiting on her targets. The skintight jeans were so tight Trigga had to help her get in them. He and Troy were parked down the street right behind Self and Bad Ass.

"Let me get a blueberry blunt wrap," Meisha told the clerk. She had to be careful when she went in her purse so no one could see the danger within.

"Sup shawty, match one?" Boobie offered. He tossed a twenty on the counter along with a couple of 60-ounce bottles of Real Nigga 9000. "I got hers too."

"Thank ya," Cameisha forced out. The thought of him paying for her stuff with her own money further inflamed her. "All I smoke is loud though. So if you ain't got none then I'll pass."

"That's all we blaze shawty!" Suspect spoke up.

"Let's ride then!" she cheered and turned toward the door. She tossed her ass generously as a going away present. A vision to take into the afterlife with them.

"Let's take her to the Motor Lodge and hit her up," Boobie suggested as they walked to the car. He and Suspect jumped in the front seat without even bothering to open the back door for their guest.

"That's what's up," Suspect agreed wholeheartedly.

"Chivalry is dead," Meisha mumbled to herself as she opened the door herself and got in. Sitting down took a little doing in those tight ass britches.

"What yo' name is?" Boobie asked as he pulled onto Glenwood. Trigga and Bad Ass pulled away from the curb as well.

"Cameisha Forrest," she replied truthfully. Why not since she was talking to dead people.

"That's my nigga Boobie and I'm Suspect."

"I bet you are," she agreed. Meisha turned around and made eye contact with Trigga. He flashed his lights in reply. When they got caught by a red light, she made her move.

"You know you guys really gotta be careful who you rob," she advised pulling the grenade then pulling the pin. She dropped it on the floorboard and jumped out. Trigga pulled up and she hopped in.

"The fuck just happened?" Suspect asked.

The grenade went off before Boobie got the chance to say he didn't know. Both men were mortally wounded from shrapnel but wouldn't live long enough to die from it. Bad Ass pulled alongside and Self jumped out.

"Remember me?" Self asked and emptied a full clip into the two men. He jumped back in the car and Bad Ass pulled away.

Mission accomplished.

Chapter 26

Desperate times call for desperate measures. Cameisha and Trigga were both desperate as they frantically searched for some dope. They wracked their brains and worked their phones looking for a connect. If not a direct connect, at least a middle man or man next to a man. Even if they had to pay thirty thousand for a kilo, they could still make a profit. Just like a shark has to keep swimming, a dealer must keep dealing.

"I may not have no choice," Trigga lamented meaning trying his luck with Belize. "Me and Troy can just take a few hoes down there and let them mule it back."

"Ok, first...you are not taking no hoes...to the Caribbean. Second, that shit is too hot. I doubt Rude Boy would even sell us anything now. I'm sure Dre told him what I told her."

"Fuck you tell her that fo'? You ain't even sure! We gotta do something!" Trigga snapped and stormed off into the bedroom. Cameisha poked her lip out from being yelled at and went back to working the phone.

Trigga searched every strip of paper in his possession until he came across Anna's card. The nerdy medical examiner's face popped into his memory. She was kinda cute but very Mexican as he recalled. A Mexican from Columbia should have a brother, or uncle, or cousin, or someone who knew someone who had some coke.

He dialed nine of ten digits before changing his mind. He remembered the shy girl and knew his charm worked better in person. Cameisha was still pouting when Trigga rushed through the living room. He knew if he came back with some work, she would get over it, quick.

****

159

"Look! Is that, that guy? That is that guy!" Brice asked and answered when Trigga pulled up and parked next to them.

"Quick!" Toshiba shouted when Trigga began to turn in their direction. She didn't want to blow their cover so she grabbed her young partner by his neck and pulled him in.

"Mmph?" Brice said when she shoved her tongue in his mouth. He caught on and played along. When she reached down and grabbed his dick, he went along and got hard in her hand. He was already in the building by the time the kiss ended.

"The guy from the airport! The boyfriend?" Toshiba said when she placed the face herself.

"Coincidence?" he asked showing that boyish naiveté that turned her on daily.

"No such thing in general and definitely not in this case. Every thing that ever happened or will happen has already been written. The boyfriend of a known Salazar associate meeting with a family member means something. But what?"

Trigga still hadn't figured out quite what to say when he got inside of the medical examiner's office. He was going to take a seat and make a plan until Anna came out of an office. She turned and walked straight at him.

Anna was slightly rattled by yet another overdose from the tainted drugs. She had tried to reach Juan for weeks since correcting the formula but he refused to return her calls. The four kilos of cocaine sat in the bottom of her closet. When she looked up and saw Trigga a smile flashed on her face then quickly disappeared. She gave him her number and he didn't call. He was possibly there about another dead person anyway, so she lifted her chin proudly, prepared to march right by him. What she didn't plan on was him flashing that smile at her.

"Hey lady, remember me?" Trigga said turning on that Trigga charm. It worked on women of all ages and hadn't failed him yet. It didn't fail on him that day either.

"No, Mr. Jackson, I do not," she shot back contradicting herself. They both heard it but he pretended not to.

"I was here a while back, my mom died. Tavarious," he explained and held out his hand.

"Anna Flores," she said failing to prevent a smile as she shook his hand.

"Can we go somewhere and talk?" Trigga asked before unhanding her hand and peering into her eyes. It's mixed signals like that, that cause problems. Especially with love-struck, nerdy, Columbian girls.

"You most certainly may take me to lunch!" Anna agreed loud enough to be heard by her co-workers. She had a date and wanted it to be known.

Trigga wasn't quite sure what to do when she extended her elbow. Luckily, she helped him out by looping her arm in his and off they went. The sexual tension in the car with Brice and Toshiba hovered like blunt smoke. Luckily, Trigga and Anna came out to break the awkward silence.

"Sho-nuff?" Toshiba announced with a confused frown when the two came out arm in arm.

"Knew he was no good for her," Brice mumbled to himself. He realized he said it out loud when his partner snapped her head in his direction. He quickly tried to clean it up. "I mean a lot of these young girls get caught up with these thugs."

"Un huh," she said in a tone making sure he knew she wasn't buying it. "I'll call Walton and see if he wants us to follow."

The cops embraced for another kiss when Trigga and Anna came near. Anna treated him to a quick glance at her crotch as he held the door open for her. He did a double take at the fat, floral print.

"Thank you," she giggled at his almost timid reaction to her fluffy rabbit.

"Um..." was all that came to Trigga's mind as the imprint imprinted on his brain. He came around and got in and pulled away.

Trigga followed Anna's turn-by-turn directions and Brice followed them. She talked non-stop like a person who didn't speak to many people. Being overprotected by so many cousins and uncles left her starved for male attention. The cops kept on driving once they pulled into a restaurant parking lot.

"I love Mexican food!" Trigga announced as they entered the Cuban establishment.

"Actually it's...me too," Anna agreed. There was no reason to correct him. He wasn't the brightest but he was rugged and handsome. She planned to fuck him, not marry him. She had been in a long sexual drought and planned to break it soon. Real soon.

The couple looked like an actual couple as they chatted and laughed over chips and salsa. They sipped sangria with their meal and chatted some more. Trigga bided his time as patiently as a girl playing double-dutch did. When the moment was right, he jumped in.

"You told me about your job, now let me tell you about mine," Trigga began then paused to be sure he had her total attention. "I'm a dope boy. I sell cocaine for a living. I know you got a brother, cousin, or somebody who sells coke. I need a connect!"

"Oh, so you're using me?" she asked rhetorically. Of course, he was and she was cool with it. Like they say, fair exchange ain't no robbery.

"Um, no, I...no," Trigga replied. The question caught him off guard.

"So you like me and friends give each other what they need?" she asked.

"Sure! Of course! Girl if you need anything from me just ask! I got cha!" he assured her.

"Remember you said that. I can get what you're looking for. How much do you pay per kilogram now?"

"Fifteen," he shot back quickly. The lowball number gave him plenty of room to negotiate but it wasn't needed.

"Ok!" Anna blurted out. The family gave her whatever she asked for but she hated having to always ask. Fifteen thousand bucks was a nice bit of play dough.

"I need ten!" Trigga shot back so loud the couple next to them turned to investigate. "Scuse me, I need ten."

"Let's start with four," Anna agreed. A new sports car popped in her head when she multiplied the fifteen grand by four. "We'll see how our friendship blossoms and take it from there."

"That's what's up. When can we do this?"

"Tonight. Come to my apartment," Anna replied.

****

"What...got...into...you?" Cameisha huffed as she struggled to catch her breath. She had to turn around to ask the question since Trigga had her bent over the arm of the sofa.

"Just missed you shawty," he replied. It was half-true but the other half had to be kept to himself. She wouldn't understand how many times Anna made his dick hard over lunch. The licking of the red lips, batting of eyes, and the way she rolled her R's.

What he didn't know was that she felt the same. Anna's panties were squishy wet in the restaurant booth. She had to lock herself in her office and masturbate as soon as she got back to work.

"I may have caught a lil' toehold. A couple of bricks, but a nigga got to jump through hoops to get them," Trigga said sadly.

"Shit, nigga do whatever you gotta do!" Cameisha cheered.

"I'on know. Four for sixty bands but she..."

"Fifteen each! Nigga you better get them shits! I got thirty on it!"

"Twenty each for you," Trigga nodded.

"Dope boy fo' real!" Meisha laughed since she always charged him full price.

Later that night Trigga followed his GPS to Anna's downtown apartment. He checked the cash in the bag and bullets in the clip before getting out of the car. The former stick up scanned all the places he would have hid had he been on a lick instead of a buy. Seeing the coast was clear, he proceeded inside.

"Right on time!" Anna cheered. His being on time meant she intended to be seen in the tiny Japanese style robe. Trigga didn't notice at first since he looked past her to survey the room for danger. By the time he got to her, he noticed she had expensive taste and nice thighs.

"I am?" he asked seeing she was fresh out of the shower. Her brown hair was wet and curly, perfectly framing her pretty face. Trigga watched her ass move under the robe as he followed her in.

"Have a seat," Anna offered as her robe came open offering a little more. She waited until his eyes ran up and down before pulling it closed and taking a seat. Even though she closed the robe, her firm thighs were still visible.

"Um, ok," he said seeing his plan to make the buy and fly, fly out the window. He planned to stay up cooking coke all night since they passed out the last of the dope that evening.

"So Trigga, you have a girlfriend?" Anna enquired. "Don't answer. It doesn't matter."

"Actually, I do," he said proudly.

"And selling cocaine benefits her, no?" she asked making her point.

"Here's the money," Trigga said putting the bag of cash on the glass table.

"The stuff is in my bedroom," she said and stood. This time when the robe opened, she didn't bother to close it. She watched his eyes trace her breasts, hard stomach, and down to the thin strip of brown pubic hair over her vagina.

Trigga sighed deeply when she turned and walked away. She switched her ass as an invitation and he stood up and followed. He remorsefully entered the bedroom recalling Cameisha's demand to do what he had to do. Anna was right, Meisha did benefit from him selling coke.

Anna dropped the robe proving Latin girls have an ass too. She gave him a peek at her freshly trimmed vagina as she climbed on the bed. It worked exactly as she planned and he was rock hard when he reached her. They made eye contact as Anna unzipped his jeans and put the erection in her mouth.

He was so excited he fought not to cum as soon as he entered her hot mouth. He fought the good fight but still lost. Anna held him in place when he exploded. The normally reserved girl planned to do all the freaky stuff she saw in the pornos she secretly watched.

"Shit! Mm, shit!" Trigga moaned and shook as she milked him dry. She held on until the spasms ceased then crawled backwards on the bed. She spread her legs wide, tacitly saying 'My turn.'

Trigga stripped and climbed between her legs. He had been with his share of women but all of them black. He took a minute to marvel at the new flavor of vagina. Anna couldn't wait another second and pulled his face into her throbbing box. Trigga knew a lot was on the line and put on. He twirled his tongue well enough to make a tornado jealous. Anna bucked and jumped with every lick. When her curses went from English to Spanish, he knew he had her.

"Sss!" Anna hissed and lifted off the bed as she came. Trigga clamped his lips on hers and went with her.

He didn't even let her recover from the violent orgasm before shoving himself inside her. Fucking her period was wrong, but raw made it worse. Only her vagina was far too hot and tight to worry about that right then.

Anna tried to run from the dick but Trigga wouldn't hear of it. She wanted to get fucked, so she was getting fucked. He held her firmly in place with one hand on her hip and the other on her ankle. She had no choice except multiple orgasms. It was over an hour later when he snatched himself out and skeeted on her stomach.

"I gotta go," he announced and jumped up. Trigga looked around and found the bathroom. He rushed in before he ended up inside of her again. He wisely avoided her frilly, fruity body wash and just used the hot water. After washing their cum off he dried off and went back in the room.

Anna was still in bed in case he wanted more. She was raw down there, but he could still have it if he wanted it. He didn't. Didn't even look at her as he put his clothes back on.

"I gotta go. The money is on the table," he repeated.

"Oh, ok!" Anna sighed, giggled, and got up. She sashayed over to her closet and gave him another look at her ass and vagina as she picked up the bag containing the four kilos.

"Can I get ten next time?" Trigga asked as he marveled at the pretty cocaine. It was so pure he could smell it though the wrapper.

"I don't know, can you?" she teased. "You keep doing it like you did and you can get a hundred!"

"I can use a hundred," he nodded. He and Cameisha planned to stack five million and retire. That would put them right there.

"My cousin Juan has more than that," Anna admitted. All that dick in her made her lose her mind and run her mouth. "He has been avoiding me for a month but I'll go to one of the stash houses and get whatever you want. Ok papi?"

"Uh, sure," Trigga said ignoring her lovesick kisses as he went towards the door. "I'll call you tomorrow."

"Ok papi. Good night, drive safe, can't wait to see you, miss..." Anna rambled until Trigga was out of sight. As soon as he was, he pulled his phone and made a call.

"Boy I got us a lick!" he exclaimed when Troy picked up.

Chapter 27

"A-yo, what's wrong with you?" Meisha asked from beneath her mask. She and Trigga had been sharing space at the stove cooking crack for an hour and he hadn't said a word. He should have been happy about the score but was withdrawn and sullen.

"Huh? Me? Nothing! I ain't did nothing!" he vowed from under his own surgical mask. Fucking Anna was eating him alive and to make matters worse, he might have to do it again. He hated that he'd enjoyed it so much.

"Ok..." Meisha replied. "I'm here for you if you need me. Love you."

The words felt like a stake through his heart. Even after she finished cooking her lone kilo, she helped him with his. They stood at the stove until the crack of dawn cooking crack. The couple cuddled when they finally hit the bed. A few hours later, they got back up to make their rounds.

Self was in the window looking like a child home alone. Cameisha couldn't help but laugh when she pulled up. She mused to herself that if he had a tail it would be wagging. She looked both ways before getting out of the car with the dope. The coast was clear, but she still walked briskly to the apartment.

"You right on time ma!" Self cheered as he let her in. Angel smiled excitedly by his side looking like she wanted to clap.

"Sup yo, hey chica," Meisha greeted with a smile of her own.

"Tell her, tell her!" Angel bounced.

"Tell me what?" she asked turning to Self. He was supposed to be relaying the good news.

"Guess what?" Self asked smugly since he had a secret.

"No," Cameisha refused with a laugh. "Just tell me."

"I'm pregnant!" Angel blurted as soon as Self opened his mouth.

"Say word! My little brudda gon' be a daddy," she teased and mussed his hair.

"Chill," he cheesed looking his age as he ducked bashfully.

"Congrats lil' mama," Meisha sang spreading her arms. Angel's eyes grew as wide as her smile and she ran over into the embrace.

"Thank you," she sang.

"You're welcome. Let me talk to my brother for a minute please."

"Ok," Angel squeezed past her smile. Once they separated, she excused herself and ran up the stairs. Cameisha waited until she was in the room before speaking.

"Sup with that other situation?" she asked low enough that the fly on the wall couldn't hear it. That way it couldn't testify about the impending murder, they were discussing.

"I'm on it. I'll be done before the weekend is out. I'm finna pick up my little whip in a few."

"Finna? Boy yo' ass is getting county as hell!" she teased. That set off a friendly banter as they got down to work. The two of them cut and bagged G-packs until Bad Ass came in and made it a threesome.

"Boy you right on time!" Bad Ass exclaimed when he saw the pile of crack on the table. He planted a kiss on Meisha's cheek and handed over a bag of cash.

Cameisha got up so Bad Ass could take over while she counted the cash. That reminded Self and he rushed upstairs to get the rest of the money. Even after the robbery, they made plenty of dough. They were not the only ones.

****

"Sho-nuff!" Troy replied incredulously as Trigga tried to recount the episode with Anna. Tried to, because Troy was stuck on the sex part.

Trigga was trying to get to the part about Juan and the stash house but his friend wanted a blow by blow about the sex. The robbery could wait; he had a more pressing question.

"Them Spanish chicks' pussy as hot as they say it is?" Troy asked pursing his lips skeptically.

"All pussy is the sa...nah, that shit was hot!" Trigga admitted. "Still, I can't believe I cheated on my girl. That shit ain't cool."

"Shit happens shawty. I accidently fucked a whole family," Troy consoled.

"Yeah, I guess. I mean, wait...what? How you accidently fuck a whole family?" he had to know.

"Well, I fucked this young girl, then her sister. They mama found out when they fought over me. She comes over calling herself checking me. I listened to what she had to say then fucked her too. Fucked her sister and her kids. Fucked..."

"Good thang they ain't had no brothers," Trigga jumped in. He tried to keep a straight face but Troy's reaction cracked him up.

"No homo shawty! Anyway, it was an accident. I ain't mean to fuck 'em all," he said and joined the laughter.

"Now comes the good part!"

"The good, hot Mexican pussy wasn't the good part!" Troy shot back. Trigga could only shake his head at his friend.

"Shawty said she got a cousin name Juan who got that work."

"Same Juan beefing with your girl? Same one who kilt Samantha?" Troy demanded.

"I'on know. He getting robbed either way," Trigga assured him.

"If it is he getting robbed and kilt!" Troy vowed.

"Fo' sho! In the meanwhile, we gonna clean them stash houses out. I'm just hoping I ain't gotta fuck that chick no more."

"I'll fuck her!" Troy volunteered like he knew he would.

"I know you will. I should've put you on her in the first place," Trigga said in hindsight. "They still getting robbed though."

****

"So what yo' girl gon' say? Or should I say baby mama," Leera dared as she slid into the passenger seat of Self's new, used car. It was the same question she asked every dude she fucked behind their girl's back. It was purely rhetorical since she didn't give a fuck. "She gon' be mad."

"Probably, if you run back and tell her," Self shot back. He pulled his car away from the curb and headed out of the complex. He drove at a quick clip to reduce the amount of people who could see her. After all, it would be the last time she was seen alive.

"Anyway," she giggled like it was a joke. "I'm glad y'all stopped blaming me for Boobie n'dem. You heard him and Suspect got kilt!"

"Nah, I ain't heard that," he replied. He didn't need to since he did it. "Probably them Jamaicans."

"That's what I heard too!" Leera lied and a rumor was born. She immediately shot a text out repeating what she'd heard. Self pulled the phone from her hand and tossed it in the backseat. The last thing he needed was her last communication saying she was with him.

"Oh, you want some attention huh?" she laughed and reached over to his lap. She fondled his dick through his jeans making it hard. "He likes me."

"He remembers that mouth," Self said hoping for a little head.

"Hmm," she hummed wickedly then gave him a little head.

Self drove into the dark park and parked. He reached into the backseat and grabbed the length of cord. After slipping it over her head, he snatched it tight. Just in time too because another minute and her mouth would have been filled with his DNA.

Leera grabbed at the cord as it cut off her air. She fought and kicked to stay alive but it wouldn't be enough. Self grunted as he literally choked her to death. He held on a full minute after her spirit left her body.

Self checked his surroundings once again before getting out. He checked once more as he came around the car. He pulled Leera's empty shell out and dragged her away. He carefully wiped her cellphone before tossing it as well. Three down, none to go.

Chapter 28

Breathe girl, Dasia mentally reminded herself. She had so much strange dick in her mouth she struggled for air. She managed to stay alive by taking sips of air into her nostrils. Luckily, for her it was one of those short, thick dicks. Had it been as long as it was wide she would have been brain damaged.

That's not to say that her brain hadn't already been damaged over the last few months of being a heroin addict. Before that, it was coke, weed, and alcohol. She'd turned her life into a drug slalom.

There's a village in every junkie's life named Rock Bottom. Every junkie will visit there at least once in their junkie career. No one actually lives there because it's not habitable. It's a catalyst that either corrects or kills. It's where Dasia and Lisa rented a room in a rundown hotel.

The North Rock motel was affectionately known as the Rocks off Inn. Home of the drive through blowjob. With so many junkie whores, they had to be creative to steer dicks into their rotten mouths and beat up boxes. Rooms rented by the month, week, day, hour, and the ever popular 'coupla minutes.'

That is where the girls retreated to once they fucked up all the money Dasia stole from her friends. They lost the condo, sold the car, and fucked that money up too. Rita and Tina stole all their clothes and were now the flyest girls in town.

This motel was where the bottom of the barrel dope fiends distributed STDs. The joint contained more viruses and bacteria than the CDC. Both Dasia and Lisa contracted HIV but neither would live long enough to die from it. In fact, they wouldn't live long enough to even get sick. Both caught it from either the dirty dicks or contaminated needles they allowed in their bodies every day.

"Mm, mm, mm," the person attached to the penis in Dasia's mouth moaned as he short stroked her face. He increased his pace signaling that the end was near. One more thrust and he filled her mouth with salty semen. She swallowed, stood, and went for the works.

Lisa stared straight up at the ceiling as a strange man stroked her insides. She was far too preoccupied with thoughts of getting high to acknowledge him. He too went into overdrive then went stiff as he came inside her. His semen joined deposits from three other men inside her rental vagina.

"Get up!" Lisa demanded pushing him off and rolling from under him. A glob of cum dropped out of her floppy vagina as she jumped to her feet. She stood over Dasia eagerly and awaited her turn with the syringe.

Dasia was forced to learn to cook and shoot her own dope during one of Lisa's frequent disappearing acts. She often left for days at a time chasing sacks.

"Hurr up," Lisa ordered as Dasia filled the dull, dirty needle. She just ignored her and found a vein to use.

"Mmm," Dasia moaned as if having an orgasm as she injected the dope into her soul. She went into a nod with the needle still in her arm. It wasn't there long because Lisa snatched it out. Not before drawing a little blood in case it still had dope in it. Yeah, it was that bad.

Lisa fixed up a shot of her own and ran it into a vein. She rocked to and fro as if listening to a soft jazz solo. A second later, she was nodding next to Dasia.

Life as a drug addict is a vicious cycle. Much like a tornado, violent and short lived. Once the high wore off, they would go off in search of the next. They were like hunters except their prey was penises. Once they trapped one, they made it hard, then soft again for a small fee.

It's a hell of a way to live. Good thing it was almost over.

****

Mo felt his dick getting harder with every step he took towards a good nut. Bilal had recently began to throw it back. He only did it to hurry the man up, but Mo loved it. Even the man had acquiesced to murder he still raped him daily. He lied to Suave and kept right on fucking the man. And since boy pussy doesn't get a menstrual cycle poor Bilal didn't get a reprieve. Until that day that is.

"You ready for me sugar?" Mo sang as he barged into Bilal's cell without asking. Bilal frowned at the intrusion that bothered him almost as much as the man barging into his anus.

"As a matter of fact I am ready for you today," Bilal replied. Had Mo not been such a scumbag pervert he would have heard the danger in his tone.

"Oh, you finally ready to give up them pretty lips huh?" Mo asked as Bilal knelt in front of him. Bilal replied by tugging his sweatpants down.

"Step out and open your legs," he directed. Mo quickly complied in preparation for some head. He closed his eyes and leaned his head back when Bilal lifted his sack. Should have kept them open and looked down so he could see what was coming.

Bilal pulled a huge shank and rammed it up Mo's ass as hard as he could. Mo was in so much pain he couldn't even yell. His mouth opened wide but nothing came out. Bilal stood and snatched the blade forward ripping through his scrotum and nearly severing his penis from the base.

"What did you do?" Mo pleaded as his testicles dropped out and dangled from the cord. He had his hands full trying to keep his package all together.

"Why, I'm killing you," Bilal replied politely. He then stuck him in his throat not so politely. Over, and over, he stabbed his neck. When Mo went down, he went with him, still sticking. "My brother wanted a killer, now he has one!"

Some of the inmates loyal to Suave heard the commotion and went to investigate. None of them wanted to try to deal with that knife so they called for help.

"Go get Lucy!" one yelled for the cop on Suave's payroll.

"What y'all got going on now?" the crooked corrections officer asked when she arrived. They pointed in the cell where Bilal had nearly decapitate Mo, twice. "Shit! Shit! Shit! Get him to the shower!"

At Lucy's direction, the crew got Bilal cleaned up. When she called the code, her fellow officers came running. In the end, the murder was put on a rival crewmember. The knife and bloody clothes were found under his bed where Lucy put them. It was big news all over the prison, but even bigger when Suave got it.

****

"My brother? Bilal? You sure? My brother?" Suave kept repeating when Lucy relayed the day's events. "My brother?"

"Yeah yeah, yeah! Your brother! Dude lost his mind. We got him in an observation room now but he's ok," she reported.

"Take him the phone. I wanna speak to him," he ordered. Lucy was an employee so she followed orders and took him the phone.

"Bilal," Lucy offered softly when she entered the room. "Your brother is on the phone."

"You're the one who wanted to give me sex aren't you?" he asked remembering her advance. She opened her mouth to respond but Bilal pounced on her.

The phone fell when he threw her face first on the bed. He held her in place with one hand and removed her uniform pants with the other. Lucy was having a not so fresh day down below but Bilal ignored it. He spit on his dick and shoved it inside her.

"What's happening? What's going on?" Suave yelled. All he could hear was their grunts and skin slapping from the rape.

Bilal didn't bother pulling out and pushed in instead. He could care less about a rape kit as he flooded her with pent up frustration. Lucy grinded against him to get it all out. Halfway through the rape she came herself.

"Tell my brother I'll be home soon, and I'm going to kill the person who destroyed my life," Bilal growled in Lucy's ear before pulling out of her.

"Okaay," she sang sounding love-struck from the good wood. She pulled her panties and pants up before relaying the message.

"Yeah, I heard him," Suave nodded approvingly. He was delighted to have broken his strong willed brother. Lucy was still talking when he hung up. It wasn't as important as his next call.

"Sup boss?" Duck asked from Atlanta.

"A-yo, we're on the way down. Time to make contact with that bitch," Suave demanded. "It's payback time."

Chapter 29

"Hey Papi I didn't expect to hear from you so soon! You must have missed me, huh? I missed you a little," Anna sang all girly and giggly when she took Trigga's call the next day. She was at work scribbling their names with hearts on the desk calendar. Her rarely used vagina was still sore and swollen from the good pounding it took the night before.

"Uh yeah...um, of course I missed you. That's why I called," Trigga said catching on. He knew he laid the pipe well and that was the result. Business and pleasure. "I need them 20 we talked about and I need to see you again."

"Well I can't wait to see it, I mean you again. I'll call my cousin and if he ignores me, again I'll just go get it from one of the houses. I get off in a few minutes and I'll call you back."

"Sounds like a plan sugar," he replied. He could hear her smiling through the line and knew he had her.

"What did she say?" Troy asked eagerly when the call ended. They were parked outside of her job in the exact same spot Brice and Toshiba had just left on their own stakeout. It wasn't much of a stakeout as all they did was flirt and talk about favorite sexual positions. It just so happened they both liked it doggy style, and who doesn't?

Inside the medical examiner's office, Anna worked the phones frantically. Her call to Juan was sent to voicemail. She tried the condo and clearly heard him tell Manny to say he wasn't there. Finally, she made a frustrated sigh and decided just to go out to the green house and get what she wanted.

"Hey babe," Trigga said taking her call.

"I'm running out to Gwinnett County to pick it up now. I'll call you when I get home and you can come get...it," she offered seductively.

"See you then," he said and clicked off. A second later, she emerged from the building marching towards her car. "There she is right there."

176

"Her! Right there! And you don't want to hit that no more?" Troy said seeing Anna for the first time. Even Trigga noticed how sexy she looked. The good sex had her feeling sexy. When a woman feels sexy, she dresses sexy. She wore a lace bra and panty set under a tight skirt and a semi sheer blouse. The 3-inch heels were a far cry from her normal flats. Big bouncy curls framed her face, which was made up with bright red lipstick. Memories of those lips on his dick the night before threatened to make him hard once more so he quickly turned away.

Anna pulled her two-year-old Audi into traffic. The car suddenly seemed old with the 60 grand in free cash sitting in her home. It was definitely time to upgrade. Troy started his car and pulled out behind her. Downtown traffic provided the perfect cover as they maneuvered through the surface streets. Suddenly they were on 85 heading north. The ride ended up in a working class subdivision in Gwinnett County.

"I'm just getting here," she said proving the house she just pulled up to was the spot. "I'll see you in a few."

"Yeah you will," Trigga replied hanging up. "She said she just got there, that's it shawty," he told Troy.

"So how you want to play it? Come back on the late night creep?"

"Nah," Trigga contemplated. There were no cars in the driveway and Anna just walked straight in. The time was now. The key to a successful stash spot is not letting it look like a stash spot. No million people in or out and no security. It appears just like any other house on the block except it contains millions in cocaine, several guns, and one hostage.

"Hola que pasa?" Chaparo asked as Anna waltzed into the house.

"Juan told me to come get some stuff," she lied. "Ten kilos."

"He did?" he asked in confusion. Juan had just been there a few hours earlier and hadn't mentioned it. He made it his business to visit his concubine often. She had the freedom to roam the house but not leave it. No phone or internet access either.

"Yes, I..." Anna began but was cut off by the masked men who burst in behind her.

"Y'all know what this is," Troy yelled from behind his AK-47. Trigga was right behind him holding a nine eye high.

"Easy papi," Chaparo offered soothingly. He knew firsthand how easily a robbery could evolve into a murder. He shot a glance at his cousin and twisted his lips knowing that she was followed.

"We easy, just come on with them keys," Troy said telling on themselves. Anna was a very smart woman and figured it out. She turned to a masked Trigga and looked him up and down.

"Tavarious?" she asked sounding wounded like she wanted to cry.

"Just business mamacita, nothing personal," he said pulling up his now useless ski mask. Troy pulled his up also just a little bit.

"What's up shawty? How you doing?" he asked flashing that smile that got him so much ass.

Chaparo took the opportunity to try to ease his gun from behind his back. He almost made it but almost doesn't count in a gunfight. Ain't no runner up. Trigga saw him and sent him into the afterlife with a headshot.

"Where's the coke?" Troy demanded now that the clock was ticking faster. Gunshots in that neighborhood were due to be reported. It was time to get the dope and get up out of there. The bedroom off the living room opened causing all head and guns to turn in that direction. Confused frowns spread across the men's faces when they saw who it was.

"Samantha?" Troy asked looking like he saw a ghost. According to his downward glance, it was a pregnant ghost.

"Troy!" she said excitedly but the reunion was interrupted by David. He rushed in the room with an Uzi.

"Die!" he screamed, closed his eyes, and fired wildly. His first shots excused Anna from life when bullets tore into her torso. A shot pierced her lonely heart killing her instantly.

Troy turned to return fire but was a split second too late. He caught five rounds in his chest. He back peddled backwards into the wall and slid down. Trigga ducked the rounds sent his way and sent a few of his own. David dropped dead with a hole in his forehead.

Trigga hated to leave empty handed but hated leaving his only friend even more. There was no time to search the house so he turned and left. He was almost to the car when he heard footsteps behind him.

"Wait for me," Samantha pleaded as she rushed to catch up. She jumped in the passenger seat as he slid behind the wheel

"Fuck, fuck, fuck!" he screamed pounding the steering wheel.

"We gotta go," she pleaded. She too knew the police would be there any second. Trigga knew she was right and pulled out of the driveway. He drove briskly out of the subdivision and hit the highway.

"My poor Troy," she whined as they drove south back towards the city.

"We thought you was dead too shawty," he said through his own tears.

****

"Hey baby I...oh my God! Oh my God oh my..." Cameisha stammered and covered her mouth when her dead friend walked in behind her man. Trigga was too distraught to find words and collapsed on the sofa. "You're alive? You're pregnant!"

"I am. Both," she replied and rushed into her embrace. Her friend held her, rocked her, and let her get it out like true friends do.

"How, what, who?" Meisha asked unable to form full questions but wanting answers.

"I don't know. Juan kidnapped me from the house months ago. Beat me up, put me in the trunk of his car, and made me make cocaine. He is the who," she said placing her hand on her small baby bump.

"He...raped you?" she asked tenderly.

"Raped...no. I did what I had to do to stay alive. This is the result," she replied leaving out how good the sex was.

"I'm still going to kill him. Where's Troy? Thought you were picking him up?" Trigga tried to speak but no words would come out.

"He's dead...David killed him..." When Trigga regained his composure, he told her the whole story. All of it.

Chapter 30

"Where you going?" Trigga asked seeing Cameisha getting dressed up. He loved watching his girl dress almost as much as he liked watching her undress. That day wasn't normal casual fly attire; she was extra. A knee length black skirt over black hose and black heels. She placed a string of faux pink pearls around her neck to match her pink mink coat.

"To your girlfriend's funeral." They had barely spoke since he told her about the sex with Anna. Oddly, she wasn't mad, but jealous.

"The hell you are!" he shot back sitting straight up on the bed.

"You right, the hell I am," she shot back. She grabbed a paper bag and headed towards the door.

"What's in the bag?" he asked giving up on telling her what to do.

"A present for the police," she chuckled at her last minute idea.

"Be careful," Samantha warned when Cameisha breezed through the living room.

"For what? I'm going to the safest place in the city today," she said on her way out the door.

Cameisha had been neglecting her Benz for fear of being seen in it. She drove it that day because that was exactly what she wanted, to be seen. It worked and she was spotted the second she pulled into the graveyard. And by more than just the Salazars.

"There's your girlfriend," Toshiba said as Cameisha stepped out of her car. Brice pouted about being teased as she radioed the news of the newcomer to Detective Walton.

Cameisha had figured correctly that the triple funeral for three of the drug clan's family members would be a big deal with the cops. The police had no idea if a war was brewing or what was happening. And what better place to strike than a family gathering. That's why there was more police there than a Police Benevolent Association ball. Not just undercover narcs but an ocean of blue to prevent an attack.

"Isn't that the girl?" a lieutenant from the drug family asked when he saw Cameisha casually strolling towards them.

Marisol had just been smiling down at Anna's casket knowing her shameful secret was about to be buried with her. Both mother and son snarled when he looked up and saw her coming.

"Dami pistola," Juan growled angrily.

"Not here," his ruthless mother reminded. A smile spread on Cameisha's face when she saw the distress on theirs. She was the enemy right there in their face and there wasn't shit they could do about it. The preacher was eulogizing the occupants of the three boxes in rapid fire Spanish when she arrived. She sarcastically crossed herself at the caskets before turning to speak.

"Hola hermano, Madre," Cameisha said trying not to crack up.

"I told you she was behind this," Marisol growled through clenched teeth. The truth of the matter was they didn't know who was behind the attempted robbery at the stash spot. All they had was a dead black man and no one to connect him to. The failed robbery left over a hundred kilos behind. Although the press conference later that evening reported only 50.

"Actually, nah, but I am going to kill the both of you the very first chance I get. Promise," she vowed and crossed herself once more.

"Not if I kill you first," Juan said practically breathing fire.

"We shall see my brother," she said before turning to Marisol. "Looking forward to seeing you in the box next and your hair looks a mess."

"Oh!" Mama Salazar said as she raised her hands to her head. She turned to her sister to comfort her vanity as Cameisha walked away.

"What the hell is going on?" Detective Walton frowned as he watched through binoculars.

"Beats me," a cop replied as he filmed the scene.

"Follow her!" both Juan and Detective Walton ordered as Meisha strolled back to her car. Knowing she had an audience, she switched her ass hard enough to make the full-length mink coat sway back and forth.

"Right away boss" both a Salazar lieutenant and Brice replied.

Cameisha laughed as she watched both of the cars pull out after her. She wondered for a second which car contained the good guys and which one held the bad guys. She got her answer a second later when a squad car pulled over the Salazar car at Toshiba's direction. If they had guns or drugs, they were going to jail. If not, they could go on their way. Either way they would not be following Cameisha today.

"Fall back, she's going to see you," Toshiba warned as Brice followed a little too closely.

"I got this I know what I'm doing," he shot back but when Meisha smiled, winked, and waved through the rearview mirror she proved him wrong.

"Just hard headed!" she scolded shaking her head.

Cameisha sang and rapped along with every song on the radio as she drove aimlessly through Atlanta. She kept an eye on her pursuers to make sure they were still behind her. When she grew tired of the cat and mouse game, she made her move to lose them. She stuck the paper bag out the window and held it for second to make sure they saw it. Once they did, she dropped it and bent a corner.

"Did you see that? I bet that's dope!" Brice exclaimed.

"Forget it, stay on her!" Toshiba ordered but he was indeed hard headed. He pulled over and ran to retrieve the bag. Cameisha just laughed at them both and mashed on the gas.

Brice grabbed the bag and snatched it open like he just made the bust of the century. All he got was his feelings hurt. He gave a disgusted scowl at the contents of the bag and tossed it down. Toshiba had her I told you so look on her face when he returned.

"Well Sherlock, what did you find out?" she quipped.

"She got her period."

Chapter 31

"Aw sookie now! Where you headed? Oh, you must got another little Spanish girlfriend," Cameisha asked seeing Trigga dressed in his grown man attire. He replaced his expensive jeans with slacks and traded his Jordans for loafers. They weren't back on the best of terms yet, but he had just earned himself some pussy that night and he didn't even know it.

"Bout to hit the Body Double," he replied smoothing his crown of thick waves with his hand.

"Body Double! Why you going there when you got all this right here?" she asked slapping an ass cheek and making it jiggle.

He certainly couldn't argue that he didn't have ample ass to look at, at home, but the mission wasn't about ass watching. The Body Double was currently the premier strip club in the city. It was where the finest dancers in the ATL worked the greasy poles. As a result, both professional and street-ballers flocked to mingle with the morally bankrupt women.

"I can only look in there, I'm touching that when I get in," he vowed.

"Okaaay," Cameisha sang signaling that the beef was over. "Make it happen captain cuz we're almost out," Meisha said. They had stretched the 4 kilos from Anna as far as they could possibly go. "Guess I'll go check on the preggos."

"How they making out over there?" he asked thoughtfully. Samantha wanted to go home after the whole ordeal but Cameisha begged her to stay. She reluctantly agreed and moved into the condo with Aqua but would not make any more of the dope. Cameisha understood and never asked her again. She thought about asking every day but never did.

"They cool," she replied and slipped into her thoughts.

"Don't worry shawty, we gon' get this bread up and move to Africa with your family," he assured her with a wet kiss to her forehead.

"That's what's up baby," she replied, not bothering to correct the continent. He was down to go with her and that was all that mattered. She planned to buy him a globe for Christmas anyway.

****

The parking lot of the high-end strip club looked like the showroom of a high-end car dealership. There was several million dollars' worth of exotic vehicles. The professional athletes had brand new imported cars with all the stock options. The dope boys had the ones they traded in 2 years ago and embellished them with all the aftermarket etceteras. Even the strippers pushed exotic whips. Some had baby seats tucked in the trunk while others had abortion receipts hidden in their glove boxes.

"Gotta pay the cost to be the boss," Trigga told Troy when they pulled into the valet parking line. When no reply came, he turned to the empty passenger seat where his right hand man should have been. Instead, he was in a box 6 feet deep.

Troy's entire family including a daddy he'd never met had been murdered in drug related crimes. It was like the ghetto version of the Kennedy curse. That fact drove home Cameisha's plan to get the money and run. He realized this wasn't the life for him because it's hard to live when you're dead. To make matters worse, they couldn't even go to the funeral. Both local and federal police were lying in wait to catch whoever Troy's accomplice was. They knew there was no way he tried to rob the drug house on his own. Not just the cops but also a Columbian hit squad ready to exact revenge. All Trigga could do was pour out a little liquor and put one in the air for his fallen partner.

"Preciate it," Trigga thanked the parking attendant as he gave up his keys along with a crisp hundred dollar bill. It took another one just like it to bypass the wanna be players in the long line and use the VIP entrance.

Trigga laughed at the street-level drug peddlers hoping to get in and rub shoulders with the big dogs. They even looked like street dealers with the loud clothes, gold teeth, and dreadlocks. These silly dudes will swear someone snitched on them when they get caught; when in fact, they tell on themselves. It's like a female dressing like a whore and expecting to be treated like a lady. If you see a man in a fireman's uniform, you would assume he was a fireman. Whore uniform; whore. Dope boy uniform; dope boy. It's not rocket science.

He spent another hundred to get the velvet rope to the VIP lifted. The booths were all full so he took one of the two empty seats at the bar. The other was filled just as he arrived. Trigga frowned at the man realizing he seen him several times already that night. Once when he left the condo then again at the gas station. Now at the bar. He felt like he was being followed. He was but when he looked at the man, he was preoccupied with the sexy strippers. Trigga shrugged it off as a healthy dose of dope boy paranoia. If you're in the streets committing crimes your ass better be paranoid because everyone is out to get you.

"What y'all drankin'?" a beautifully uncovered white bartender asked looking between the two newcomers. Both of their eyes shot straight down to her big breasts as if they asked the question. The big, pretty melons were bare except for pasties covering the big brown nipples. Trigga had a sudden craving for milk.

"Cognac," the man said. He had the odd accent of someone from New York who lived in the south for a long time. Sounds kinda like a cat barking or a dog saying meow.

"Same here," Trigga announced before she turned to leave. They both shot their eyes down to her ass as it jiggled away.

"And niggas be saying white girls ain't got no ass," he remarked.

"They a damn lie!" Trigga said in defense of white girls with booty. They both laughed and slapped five because a fat ass does deserve a high five. "I'm Trigga."

"Montel, but call me Nut," he replied offering his hand. "You must be in the music business? No way you're one of these wanna be Bama ass dope boys in here."

"I can't rap a lick!" Trigga laughed. "I ain't a Bama either but I am a dope boy." Trigga had sized the man up and quickly ascertained that he was working with some dough. He had seen the same watch on his wrist in the store and knew the diamonds were real. It ran just south of ten grand. The clip that held his stack of brand new hundreds was pure platinum.

"Shit me too, I guess. More of a broker or middleman. My people got so much of the stuff I make a nice commission off it," Nut explained. That part was true even if everything after was a lie.

"So what them thangs going for? I need as many as I can get my hands on."

"10 grand if you're getting 50 or better," Nut replied casually. As if fifty bricks of cocaine was nothing.

"50!" he shouted and then sipped his liquor to play it off. "50 is good but I'm going to need like about 10 to start."

"We don't really do nothing under 50 but fuck it, for you 17.5."

"Shit after I flip them 10 bricks a couple of times I'll fuck with you on the 50. Half a mil is a sweet ticket!" Trigger said hopefully.

"It is sweet but check it," Nut said and paused for effect. "The people I fuck with are very, very serious. You seem like a cool dude, they ain't. If you ain't straight up and down and I mean like 6 o'clock then you better off fucking with...him."

Trigga looked at the gold-toothed dope boy wearing bright orange everything and laughed. He was dipped in 10-carat chains with cloudy, slum diamonds. You just knew he had an old school donk outside sitting high on big ass rims.

"Shawty I'm a businessman. Sell me 10 kilos and I'll be back in a few days for 10 more. Give me a month or so and I'll be ready for them 50," he vowed.

****

"Where you think you going?" Trigga asked as Cameisha stood to follow him out.

"With my money," she shot back since half of the one hundred and seventy five thousand dollars in the bag was hers. She wasn't in the mood to take any more losses and tucked a pistol in her purse to prove it.

"I got this shawty. Dude lives downtown too, a few blocks away from here. I'm going to his crib," he said trying to dissuade her.

"Mm hmm," she replied unmoved.

Trigga knew his girl well enough to know she wasn't giving up or giving in. The makeup sex they had after the club was great but that was personal and this was business. He twisted his lips, shook his head, and held his tongue. She was coming too. They pulled out of the underground parking and hit Peachtree Street. A few streets later, they pulled into the underground parking of yet another high-rise building. Their eyes quickly covered every square inch of the parking area searching for danger. Seeing none, Trigga put the car in park and they got out and walked to the elevator.

"A-yo if we get 50 bricks we'll clear over 2 million," Cameisha whispered as they ascended. "Shit that's more than enough!"

"Is it?" he wondered aloud. That was one of the dope boy curses; it's never enough. Make one million you want two, make two million and you want 10. Some hustlers can shift gears into legitimate ventures but some can't. Dope boy for life.

"Guess we'll find out huh?" Meisha replied as the door open on Nut's floor.

The plush unit was courtesy of Suave, who had one of his own on the top level. He would be living in it in a couple of weeks when his brother got out of prison.

"Here we go," Trigga announced halfway down the thickly carpeted hallway. He rang the doorbell and stood in front of the peephole, which was actually a camera.

"Who?" Nut barked from behind the door. The rhetorical question was out of habit since he already knew exactly who it was. He opened the door with a smile that quickly changed into a frown. "Who is this?"

"My bad shawty, this is my girl Cameisha. She's in the bag with me," he explained meaning that half of the money in the bag belonged to her.

"Sup," Nut said and stepped aside so they could enter. He shot a quick glance down at her fat ass as she passed. He didn't want to cross the thin line between respect and disrespect. That could lead to an argument that would lead to a fight that would bring out the gunman in the back and end in a gunfight. And that would disobey Suave's order that no one made a move without him.

"Nice place," Cameisha nodded as they entered.

"Thanks; have a seat," the host offered gesturing towards the sofa.

"Count that," Trigga said sitting the bag of cash on top of the table that separated them.

"May as well blaze while we work," Nut said lighting a blunt. He took the customary two pulls and passed it over. When Trigger accepted the blunt he began running the cash through a money counter. The sound of the money machine was hypnotic and had them both entranced.

"I like your style son," Nut smiled and nodded as the final cut was over instead of under. He slid the change across the table and stood to go get the dope.

"That's mine!" Cameisha shouted and snatched up the extra cash before Trigga could get it. Nut returned with the coke a minute later and set it on the table. They could smell the cocaine through the wrapper and knew it was that shit.

"Check it shawty, we run all our shit through the trap so it'll be a couple days, week at the most," Trigga explained as he put the coke in the bag the cash just came out of.

"That's a bet," Nut said and exchanged a pound with him and a head nod with her. He took one more mental snapshot of her ass as she left. The phone rang the second he closed the door behind them. It was almost like they were being watched, because they were.

"Damn that little bitch is fine! No wonder she had little bro all fucked up," Suave said watching the transaction through the security cameras. "I may have to hit that my damn self!"

Chapter 32

"Won't be long now," Meisha said rubbing Aqua's big belly like a crystal ball. The baby inside moved against her hands in response.

"I wish. I can't wait to see my Stevie again," Aqua pouted.

"How do you know it's a boy?" Samantha asked and to everyone's surprise stopped talking. It was proof that you can break a person. Juan's beatings had knocked all the extra talk out of the girl.

"Oh, I just know," Aqua responded so surely no one doubted her. The answer was followed by a dense silence that indicated something serious was coming. Cameisha mulled over her words carefully before turning to Samantha.

"So Sam, ummm..."

"I'm keeping it," Samantha blurted knowing where she was going. "He or she has nothing to do with him."

"Well you do understand that 'him' is about to be dead, don't you?" Cameisha asked. Samantha just shrugged and sipped her milk.

"So when you and Trigga going to have some babies?" Aqua wanted to know once again.

"Chile, please, ain't nobody got time for that," Meisha laughed. The fake laugh was despite her wondering where her period was. It should have come days ago so she had worn a pad for whenever it decided to show up. She was on the pills but the funny thing about them is you have to actually take them for them to be effective. She would miss a couple days then swallow three or four pills to make up. "Probably just stress."

"What is?" Samantha asked cocking her head curiously.

"Huh? Oh nothing," she said realizing that she had thought out loud. "Anywho, let me go to check the trap."

Cameisha planted wet kisses on her friends' foreheads and got broad smiles in return. She was so consumed by her thoughts that she didn't even turn on the radio as she drove. For the first time she no-

191

ticed how drastically, the scenery changed from downtown Decatur to the hood. The freshly painted houses with manicured lawns gave way to liquor stores and pawnshops.

The happy, smiling black and white faces were replaced by exclusively black downtrodden hopeless ones as soon as she crossed Memorial Drive. An old drunk lady danced on the corner to music no one else could hear. Soulless zombies roamed the streets in search of a chemical escape. They would gladly trade cash or flesh for the next get high.

Legions of young black boys stood in every parking lot with drugs and guns in baggy pants. They all dressed alike, acted alike, talked alike, and shared the same common fate. None of them would ever achieve the riches their favorite rappers lied about in songs and videos. The rappers rapped, for them it really was get rich or die trying. Many would make revolutions through the revolving doors of the state's prisons. They would continue catching two and three years skid bids until they earned recidivist status and got their socks knocked off with 30 or 40-year bids. Quite a few more would die out there in those streets.

People always say black people have the crabs in the barrel mentality but that's not true. Crabs are far more humane. They won't murder you for what's in your pocket or for the right to sell crack on a particular corner. The police loved the black on black crime. They called them two for one specials. One black men dead and another one in prison was a win-win situation for them. It's funny how black people rally, loot, hoop, and holler when the police kill a black man but no one is concerned when Paco killed Mook-Mook. Where's his rally? Where's his protest and marches?

The fatherless children are left behind; doomed to repeat the vicious cycle of life and death in the hood. Cameisha tried to swat the fly that landed on her face, but when it splashed, she realized it was a tear. What started out as a lone tear was quickly followed by many many more. She was suddenly overwhelmed and began bawling like a wet, hungry, lonely, project baby. When she pulled into Eastwyck, she tried to man up and get herself together. She lifted her shirt and dried her face before going into the apartment.

"What's wrong with you?" Self asked as if he was angry at whatever had her so distraught.

"Nothing, I'm cool; what we looking like?" she said trying to deflect the attention away from her.

"Looking like some rich niggas! The trap is booming. I put them niggas on Glenwood down and they on point too. If they fuck up I'm going to go over there and air that shit out," he said demonstrating his new taste for murder.

"I know that's right...Wait! No, if they come up short cut 'em off," she said catching herself. It was like the voice inside of her said no more killing.

"Huh?" he asked in confusion. He knew full well she was a killer and would kill about her money.

"You heard me; no more killing. If niggas want to bite the hand that feeds them then fuck them, they don't eat. Let them starve out this bitch!" she shot back trying to sound tough. Self looked at her oddly wondering what had changed. He couldn't see it because changes of the heart are invisible to the naked eye.

Between Trigga and Cameisha, the 10 kilos were gone in ten days. Ten days later, they ran through another 10 keys and then did it again. It was now time to make the buy that would set them straight for life. With Troy living on in memories and t-shirts, Trigga had to make all the pickups and drop-offs by himself. After Snake, no one ever came short again. The chicken heads never even looked his way since he never even gave them the time of day.

Of course, they could have moved the dope a lot quicker by selling wholesale but at a much smaller profit. Instead they grinded nick by nick and dime by dime until they had the half a million dollars that they needed. They were all set for their happily ever after until Bilal came home.

Chapter 33

"Well, well, well look at my baby bro," Suave clapped as Bilal stepped off the bus. Amber and Darla also clapped and bounced by his side.

"What are you doing here?" Bilal asked with his displeasure written all over his face.

"My baby brother fresh out from a bid, you know I had to be here! Not like when I got home and you were off playing doctor. But we're not going to go there right now. Besides you're paroling out to my address so I'm responsible for you," Suave said. He came over and put his arm around him to lead him to the car.

"I don't know why we're here. You think that girl is going to show up? After he went to prison for her?" Brice asked as he and Toshiba waited on Bilal's return as well.

"I doubt it but you know your boss, he likes to cross all the Is and dot all the Ts," she replied. Toshiba shot her partner a side eye scowl seeing him oogling the white girls following the men to their car. "You like what you see? What is it with you black men and white women?"

"White girl head. Eighth wonder of the world," he said not blinking from Amber and Darla's ample asses.

"Whatever!" she laughed at yet another silly stereotype. She started the car and discretely followed them to the high rise. That address got put on their stake out list too.

****

"Wow!" was all Cameisha could come up with when her count confirmed what Trigga had. The cash on the table in front of them equaled a half million dollars.

"Wow is right!" he agreed.

"A-yo, let's take the money and run! We won, let's just go!" she suggested. The money would be worth three or four times that amount in

194

South America. Not to mention Self was straight. He had cash stacked to the ceiling. Jackie had damn near every dope dollar she ever made. Aqua and Samantha were together. Bad Ass tricked his off but he was cool too.

"Shit shawty, we flip this and we gone be super straight!" Trigga replied. It was that old dope boy curse once more. One more score, one more flip. How many tombstones should that phrase be on? Either that or 'died trying'.

"You right," she agreed since the dope boy curse affects dope girls too. "Make the call. I got to use the bathroom."

When Cameisha got into the room, she retrieved her recent purchase hidden in the closet. The bankbooks left by her dope boy father caught her eye. The worthless books contained only numbers and no name. It was all that he had left behind as far as she knew. What she did not know about the trust funds was that they were in every one of his kids' names. They were straight for life.

"Stop procrastinating and handle your business," she heard herself say and got up. She went into the bathroom opened the box and read the directions aloud.

"Pee on stick and wait 15 minutes...That's it?" she asked the box. It seemed like something so important would be a little more difficult.

"Say shawty, come on. He ready now!" Trigga yelled from the front of the condo. He had just hung up with Nut who had told him to come now.

"Give me 12 minutes!" she shouted back.

"Man, I'll be back by then I'm finna go!" he insisted and hit the door. Cameisha was on his ass before he reached the elevator.

"I can't believe you were going to leave me," she pouted as she caught up. She left the test strip on the counter in a rush to grab her gun.

"What's in there?" he asked even though he already knew it was a gun. They had done business so many times before he felt like he could trust Nut. In this business that's called getting rocked to sleep.

"A Mac and I don't mean lip-gloss" she shot back. Cameisha was taught by the best and she didn't take naps. Especially with a half a million at stake.

****

"So you ever do anal?" Toshiba asked as they sat in the garage of Suave's high-rise. As usual their stake out was filled with sexual banter.

"Yuck! No!" Brice grimaced.

"Me neither," Toshiba said seeing his aversion. "Here's our new friends."

"Where to now? The barbershop? A restaurant?" he said since most of their surveillance went nowhere. He prepared to start the car and follow.

"Dude is out of it," she couldn't help but notice as Bilal followed in a zombie like state. He was even like that when his brother sicced Amber and Darla on him. He would just stare off into space while they tag team blew him.

"Looks like he's walking the plank," Brice noticed. He has an odd dead man walking look in his blank eyes. They got into the SUV but didn't move. It was like they were on a stake out of their own. Or an ambush.

"The plot thickens, isn't that the boyfriend?" Brice asked when Trigga pulled into the garage.

"And the girl. What the hell is going on here?" Toshiba asked but didn't wait for an answer. "I'm calling it in."

"Fifty bricks!" Trigga announced triumphantly as he pulled into the underground parking lot. A score like that was every dope boy's dream and there he was.

"Welcome to the big leagues baby," Cameisha cheered and raised her hand for a high five.

"You ready to handle yo' business nigga?" Suave asked when they saw Cameisha. Bilal looked at the gun for a few seconds before accepting it.

"I'm ready to kill the person responsible for ruining my life," he said with the enthusiasm of someone who had been brainwashed. He took a deep breath like one does at the top of the high dive, held it, and then jumped.

Cameisha registered someone approaching behind Trigga and craned her neck to see around him. When she and Bilal locked eyes, she struggled to place the face. His being there, made absolutely no sense. She saw the gun at the exact same moment as Toshiba.

"Gun!" Cameisha and the cop yelled at the same time. Trigga turned just as Bilal raised the gun and fired.

The glass shattered as the bullet passed through and slammed into Trigga's temple. Cameisha was sprayed by the glass and blood as he slumped over.

"Noooooo!" she screamed and jumped out with the Mac 10. Before she could shoot Bilal, he smiled and put the barrel in his mouth. With a quick tug on the trigger, he killed the person responsible for ruining his life.

"No you didn't! You little bitch; you were supposed to kill her! You bitch," Suave fumed as he jumped out with his own gun.

"Drop the guns!" Toshiba shouted as she too jumped out. She moved her gun back and forth between the two armed people but Brice hadn't budged. She looked at Brice in the car and he was frozen in place by the explosion of violence.

Suave raised his gun and rushed towards Cameisha. He made it a whole two steps before she sent him running backwards with a three shot burst into his chest.

"Put it down!" Toshiba ordered once more. She made the fatal mistake of looking at her partner once more.

Cameisha took advantage of the pause and sent shots her way as well. Toshiba wore a vest but it didn't cover her face. A .45-caliber slug ran through her mind like an idea and ended her life as well. Brice sat there shaking like a leaf. Cameisha dropped the gun and jumped into the truck Suave got out of. He certainly couldn't drive it to hell.

"Oh Trigga," Cameisha wailed as she pulled out of the garage. Luckily, police didn't have a description of the truck and she drove right past them as they arrived.

Cameisha knew the contents of the car would lead the police to the apartment. She allotted herself five minutes inside and grabbed everything she could. She stuffed a couple of pairs of panties along with all the extra cash into a tote bag. She tossed in the bankbooks and then grabbed the pink mink coat, which was the first gift that Trigga ever bought her.

With two minutes to spare, she rushed into the bathroom and sat on the toilet. And as if things weren't bad enough, the pregnancy test had a pink plus sign. Cameisha was pregnant.

****

"What? What?" Samantha screamed when Cameisha rushed in the condo yelling incoherently. Her hair was wild and she had dried blood on her face.

"Trigga, Bilal, cops, dead. They're all dead!" Meisha managed. She was out of breath from the murders and sprint from the parking lot. Once fully inside, she sank to the floor and sobbed.

"Huh?" Aqua asked as she came and sat on the floor next to her. She wrapped her in her big arms and rocked her gently. "What happened?"

"I don't know! Bilal was there. He shot Trigga then the cops came and some other man," Cameisha rambled trying to make sense of what just happened.

"Did you pee?" Samantha asked Aqua as a puddle formed under her.

"No! I think my damn water broke!" she said referring to her amniotic fluid.

"I'll call an ambulance!" Samantha exclaimed and made the call. A call of a woman in labor in that neighborhood was answered immediately. Moments after she hung up paramedics were knocking on the door. Cameisha rushed into one of the bedrooms so she wouldn't be seen.

"Just relax, everything will be fine," the EMS worker offered in a calm soothing tone when Samantha let him in. He had a pleasant Midwest twang to his speech.

"Not me, her," she said pointing to Aqua on the floor. The man's face and demeanor changed instantly.

"You got insurance?" he demanded now sounding like he was from Brooklyn.

"Huh?" Aqua replied which meant no. "It's a baby not a car! Duh!"

"Grady," the two EMS techs said in unison. Grady Hospital was the state run facility for the poor and uninsured.

Coincidentally it had the best trauma center in the southeast. Being located in the heart of an extremely violent city, it specialized in gunshot wounds. That's why Trigga was transported there when it was discovered that he had a pulse. He was one of three headshots that day. One was pronounced dead on arrival while he and another man clung to life.

Cameisha had no way of knowing he survived the attack. Once she was alone in the apartment, she made the decision to join him in death. She put the barrel in her own mouth just as Bilal did and pulled the trigger.

"Fuck!" she screamed when it didn't fire. A quick check showed the safety was on. She took it off safety ready to try again when Aqua's phone buzzed on the dresser. Curiosity got the best of her and she checked the message. It was Dasia saying, "I need some money."

'What's your address?' Meisha texted back as a new plan formed. She still intended to join Trigga but planned to take a few more people with them.

Chapter 34

"What the fuck are you doing here?" Big Shawn grumbled when he found Cameisha sitting in his living room at 3 am. He didn't bother asking how she got in since her uncle Killa always pulled the same stunt.

"Sorry for the intrusion but...I need that thing. Sampson," she explained with the soft cadence of the condemned.

"Sampson? No! For what?" Shawn shouted at the odd request. "It's not for sale."

"Then I won't buy it," she explained and produced a pistol. "Just say I robbed you. I can shoot you in the ass if you want? You know, to make it more believable."

"That won't be necessary," he assured her and led her into the show room. Cameisha walked straight over to the mannequin and fondled the device.

"Will this thing go through mink?" she wondered.

"Mink? It'll go through a tank! It's a bomb," he said to the odd question

"Is it...on? You know, ready to go?" Meisha asked hauntingly.

"Uh...yeah. All set, just press the red button." he replied quite unbelievably.

"This one?" she asked as she pressed it. As she expected, nothing happened. Didn't make her a difference since she planned to die anyway. "You sure you don't need me to shoot you in your ass?"

"Your uncle is going to kill me for this," he sighed as he armed the suicide vest. He connected some wires, hit a switch, and backed away gingerly.

"You sure it's on this time?" she asked grabbing the detonator. The big man dove to the floor and balled up. "I'll take that as a yes."

****

201

"Ok...so, tell me again what happened?" Detective Walton asked Brice in a calm his comrades knew to be false. The room full of police officers had just watched the security footage from the garage and it didn't match the story he gave. According to the tape, Toshiba died because Brice was a coward. He choked in battle and got his partner killed.

"I um..." he began before being cut off by a vicious backhand slap. Walton snatched him by his collar and yelled inches from his face.

"You fucking coward!" he screamed spewing tobacco flavored saliva in Brice's face. "The prints came back off the murder weapon. Your girlfriend killed a motel clerk in Mississippi. She's a cold blooded killer!"

The rest of the cops present were too sad and angry to intervene. The ass chewing ended up with him being dismissed with a kick in his ass.

"This...girl...is wanted for a double homicide including one of our own. I want her found. Dead or alive; I want her found," he said. The police all nodded in favor of dead.

Cameisha was officially public enemy number one. Pictures of her were in every squad car in the city. She was also the top headlines on the nightly news.

****

"Oh Cameisha!" Jackie wailed when she saw her friend's face splash across her TV screen.

"Isn't that your friend?" Ralph asked in shock

"Shush! Let me hear it!"

A massive manhunt is on for Cameisha Forrest seen here in surveillance footage. She is wanted in connection with a double homicide including a police officer. She's also wanted in Mississippi on a cold case murder. She's considered armed and extremely dangerous...'

"Damn Meish," Jackie sighed as tears fell from her eyes. No way was she getting out of that one. It was the end of the Dope Girl. She wasn't the only one watching the news who knew her personally.

"See! I knew she was a criminal!" Marisol shouted triumphantly to the other women in the salon. It set off a round of gossip and cackling amongst the old Spanish hens.

"I'll go grab an espresso," El Capitan announced now that he could relax. He had been assigned to round the clock security, but the girl was in too much trouble to be worrying about her. Besides the massage parlor had excellent expresso to go with the blowjobs.

Cameisha smiled as she watched the man she knew to be Mama Salazar's private security leave the shop. It saved her a bullet because she planned to put one right in his large head. She donned a big blonde wig and stunna shades that covered her face.

No one paid much attention to her as she eased into the shop. She looked around and didn't see her but heard her bitching from the back.

"Yes ma'am, sorry ma'am," the innocent shampoo clerk said getting chewed out for nothing. The girl heard the click of the switchblade open behind her.

"Sh," Cameisha whispered with a finger to her lips. The girl raised her hands and backed away. She took her place and slipped the blade under her neck. Cameisha could feel the flesh, cartilage, and veins give way as she ran the super sharp blade and cut the woman's throat from ear to big ass ear.

Marisol spun around when she realized what had just happened. She practically strangled herself trying in vain to keep her blood in her veins. It was futile and blood skeeted and spewed between her fingers. Cameisha smiled as they locked eyes. She dropped to her knees then fell on her face. Meisha stepped over her like a puddle and left the shop.

El Capitan walked out of the massage parlor happy and relaxed from his happy ending. It was short lived when he saw the commotion at the beauty salon. He just shook his head woefully when he saw Marisol stretched out. He decided to cut to the chase and removed his gun. He crossed himself and then fired a bullet into his own temple.

Chapter 35

Cameisha crossed the first name off her list and knew the clock had started. She had to rush and kill the next one so she could get back to the main event. Aqua's phone buzzed with a message from Samantha's phone but she wasn't interested. She looked at the address once more and tossed it into the back of the truck. All it said was that Trigga was still alive and Aqua had a boy. Cameisha decided that she and Trigga were the Romeo and Juliet of the hood. She was in such a hurry she refused to pull over to use the bathroom. Just peed her pants and kept on driving.

"Damn!" Cameisha said as she pulled into the rundown motel. .Actually it was now just a 'mote' since the L fell off and no one was going to fix it.

She looked on in utter disgust at the sad addicts scurrying around like forest creatures. She looked at the small scar between her thumb and forefinger and remembered the baby possum who gave it to her. It played dead and when she relaxed, it bit her.

A car door opened and caught her attention. A skinny addict stuck her skinny head out and spit a mouthful of thick semen on the asphalt. She got out and looked right through Cameisha then scurried away.

"Dasia?" Cameisha said when it registered who it was. She got out and followed her to the room.

Lisa waved her free hand when Dasia walked in. She had a mouth full of dick and couldn't speak. Two humps later, she had a mouthful of cum. She swallowed in a loud gulp and pushed it away. She scrambled over to Dasia so they could fix their next fix.

"Damn, I shoulda got you!" the trick said as he passed Cameisha in the doorway. The two junkies were so busy cooking the dope they didn't even hear their murderer enter the room.

Meisha watched in horror at what had become of her friend. They frantically fixed up shots in dirty needles to get high. It wasn't until Lisa tied her arm off that she looked up and saw Cameisha.

"What are you doing here? She's mine! Mine you hear!" Lisa shouted and got shot. Cameisha raised the pistol and fired right into her forehead.

"I'm so happy to see you," Dasia said in the utter exhaustion that is an addict's existence. It's a hard life; death would be so much easier. She was pregnant, HIV positive, and had an amazing array of STDs co-existing in her beat up vagina.

"You are?" she asked feeling a tear run down her face.

"Yes. I'm ready to go. I love you Meisha-Meisha," Dasia said and dropped her head.

"I love you too," she replied and raised the gun once more.

****

"Fuck the police, I want her found! Find her and bring her to me," Juan growled as he stood over his mother's casket.

"We'll find her," Manny assured him. No sooner did the words leave his mouth did he look up and see her. He wasn't the only one who spotted her. The blonde wig and shades disguised the face but the pink mink coat was a dead giveaway.

"This bitch has balls! Huge, gorilla, King Kong sized balls!" Detective Walton said as he saw her walking towards the gravesite full of angry Colombians. The security cameras in the salon captured that murder too so they knew she was responsible.

"Yo kill her right there on the spot," Manny ordered.

"Here? Now?" the worker questioned looking at all the police around. It was a kill or be killed order so he had no choice.

"Wait, she's coming here. I want to look in her eyes when she dies," Juan said granting her a brief reprieve.

All eyes watched the swaying mink coat as it neared the entire Salazar clan. When she arrived the shades went up, the mouth smiled, and Juan frowned. He opened his mouth to ask a question but ran out of time. His brain gave the command to run when it registered the detonator but it was too late. The 20 pounds of Simtex growled and grumbled for a millisecond before exploding. The blast vaporized everyone within a 10-foot radius. More died as the nuts, bolts, nails, and screws that packed the device spread out a thousand feet per second.

"Damn that bitch had balls!" Walton repeated himself. He actually clapped his hands proudly at how she took her enemies with her. "That was so gangsta!"

That was the end of the Dope Girl.

The end.

Epilogue

Jackie was absolutely inconsolable at Cameisha's funeral. The rented preacher did his best to speak over her wails and sobs. It really didn't matter what he was saying since he was lying. First of all, he never met the girl and second she was not the sweet little angel he portrayed her to be; despite looking like one in the picture beside the casket.

Self held his Angel under his arm as she cried a river. Bad Ass wore an angry scowl, mad because there was no one to get revenge on. Cameisha took them all out with her.

Samantha had a million things to say but said nothing. She just stared at the closed casket and wept quietly. Everyone was broken up, except Aqua that is.

She stood there rocking her brand new baby boy with a knowing smirk on the corner of her mouth. A 30 something year old lady escorted a small boy to the casket. They stood there quietly talking to the occupant before turning to leave. They stopped to hug and kiss Aqua before they left as quietly as they came.

"Who was that?" Jackie managed through her tears. She had never seen the woman before but it was obvious that Aqua knew her well.

"Saleria," Aqua replied as if just saying her name explained it. Seeing it didn't register, she expounded. "Dasia's mom and son."

"Dasia's mom? Why would she...no! Un uh!" she shouted and looked at the casket. A slow smile spread on her face as it came together. "So...who's that?"

"I'on know?" Aqua said looking at the handsome stranger who arrived. She couldn't answer that since she'd never met Cameron Forrest before. She had heard of him though, err body had heard of the Dope Boy.

****

207

A blind man walked on the marble floors of the international bank of Brazil. On his arm was a gorgeous woman with short curly hair and sun-bronzed skin. She escorted him to a chair and approached the counter.

"English, Spanish, or Portuguese?" the lovely teller requested ready to accommodate the new customer.

"English please," she said as she presented the numbered bankbooks. "Can you please tell me the balance?"

The woman entered the numbers and tapped into a calculator. Once she had the tally, she looked up and announced, "With accrued interest the total is eight million dollars."

The customer nodded approvingly and made a withdrawal of ten thousand US dollars. The blind man smiled when he heard her heels clicking towards him on the marble and got a whiff of her scent.

"Come on, Trigga, let's go shopping."

"Sure my darling, Cameisha," he said taking her elbow and rubbing her protruding belly.

"No, Cameisha is dead. Call me Tywanna."